ETERNAL REST
BED AND BREAKFAST

PARANORMAL COZY MYSTERIES

BETH DOLGNER

Scenic Views
Eternal Rest Bed and Breakfast Book Four
© 2022 Beth Dolgner

ISBN-13: 978-1-7365724-7-4

Published by Redglare Press
Cover by Dark Mojo Designs
Print Formatting by The Madd Formatter

BethDolgner.com

1

The cardboard box started to slip out of Emily's grasp, and she froze in place. She had just put one foot on the next stair up, her back leg holding her weight as well as that of the box full of antiques. Carefully, Emily tried to wiggle her fingers back into place. She felt the contents of the box shift, and she rocked back slightly to keep it balanced.

"It's okay," she told herself, her voice a higher pitch than normal. "You're not going to fall down the stairs. The box isn't going to fall down the stairs, either."

It did just that.

The heavy items inside slid a little more to one side, enough that Emily knew it was either drop the box or give up her solid footing and go tumbling down the stairs herself. She tried to control the box on its way to the ground, hoping it might balance on one of the stairs, but it ripped itself out of her grasp and went bouncing down toward the hallway below. Emily winced each time the box clanged against a step on its descent. Thankfully, she hadn't even made it halfway up the stairs yet, so the box didn't have too far to fall before it came to rest with one last thud that echoed through the hallway.

Emily groaned as she walked down to inspect the damage. She absent-mindedly brushed a lock of light-brown hair, which had escaped her ponytail, out of her face while grumbling, "I should have taken Trevor up on his offer to help."

The box had landed upright, the tape across the top flaps barely clinging to the cardboard. Emily sat on the bottom stair and gave the tape a tug, then held her breath as she opened the box. Nothing looked broken at a glance, and Emily was glad she had mostly bought pieces that could take a bit of a beating. The iron lamp didn't have a shade or a bulb yet, so it was fine. The brass bowls she had gotten to put potpourri in were similarly undamaged. Emily continued inspecting items and was relieved to find the only casualty was a cut-glass flower vase that now had a chip in the rim.

Well, Emily thought, *I can turn that side to the wall and make sure a well-placed leaf covers it up.*

Leaving the box where it was, Emily gathered up the bowls and the vase and carried them up the stairs. She knew she should have broken up the load to begin with, and she chastised herself for not being smarter. Again, she realized it would have been prudent to accept Trevor's help. He had been so sweet to offer, yet Emily had stubbornly refused his assistance. She wasn't even sure why.

Emily had just finished her third run up the stairs when her cell phone rang. She sank into a chair in one of the front guest rooms and answered with, "Are your ears burning?"

"Oh, are you gossiping about me?" Trevor asked teasingly.

"No, I was just kicking myself for not letting you help me move these new antiques into the house. I just dropped a whole box-load down the stairs. No major damage, at least."

"Want me to come over?"

"No. I'm about done now. I just have to lug that big mirror up."

"The full-length gilt floor mirror that you said is so heavy it could probably survive a tornado?" Trevor asked.

"Yeah, that one."

"Seriously, Emily, I'm happy to come over and help."

The logical side of Emily's brain was fighting with her emotional side. Yes, it would be easier to have Trevor's help, but at the same time, she didn't want to seem... what?

I don't want to seem like I need a man to help me get through life.

The unexpected thought hit Emily hard, and she was silent for so long Trevor finally said, "Emily, you still there?"

There's nothing wrong with asking a friend for help, Emily told herself. Even as she was thinking that, she heard herself saying, "Yeah, I'm still here. Don't worry, I'll be fine. I'll put the mirror down on each step. It will be slow-going, but I won't get tired or off-balance that way."

Emily could hear the concern in Trevor's voice as he said, "Okay. Well, I was calling again to ask if we can move tomorrow's lunch to one o'clock. I know we just made our plans half an hour ago, but I found out we've got a client coming in the morning, and I think the meeting will go past noon. Does that work for you?"

"Of course. I'll see you at one! Then you can lecture me in person about doing this all by myself."

Emily said goodbye and hung up the phone, still trying to figure out her strange feelings. She had been so grateful for help right after Scott died, accepting offers for everything from taking out the trash to help cleaning guest rooms. She wasn't sure what she was suddenly trying to prove to the world.

"And, goodness knows, I need help," Emily said out loud. Her guests at Eternal Rest Bed and Breakfast that weekend had checked out by noon, and Emily had cleaned the rooms—all four had been booked—before she had driven into Oak Hill to shop at Everything Old is New Again. She wanted to spruce up the rooms a bit, and she could easily justify the expense since business was so good. The ornate floor mirror had been a real splurge, but it was such a perfect fit for a Victorian home that Emily couldn't pass it up.

Emily grabbed the now-empty box from the foot of the stairs and took it out to the recycling bin next to the back steps. She had already unloaded the mirror from the back of her car, where it had barely fit, and moved it to the bottom of the steps. She had to wrap her arms around it in an awkward sort of bear hug to lift it, and as she had promised Trevor, she moved it up onto just one step. She repeated the process three more times before it was up the back steps and inside the house. *Progress,* Emily told herself. Eventually, she had the mirror in place in one corner of the guest room just above the parlor. The room had felt off to her ever since one of her guests, Jaxon Knight-MacGinn, had snuck out from there one night, only to get himself killed. It was like some lingering negativity, either from Jaxon's personality or from the events surrounding his murder, was still there in the room. Even after saging the house to clear out negative energy, Emily still felt uncomfortable in the space.

The mirror helped the room feel refreshed and different. Emily tilted it so it reflected the sunshine into the room. The brightness of the reflection and the shine of the gilt frame instantly improved the atmosphere.

With all the antiques she had bought finally in place and the rooms ready for the next round of guests, Emily felt satisfied but also sticky. It was only late May, though it seemed that summer had decided to show up early. The humidity had made hauling the antiques sweaty work.

By the time Emily was showered, dressed in fresh clothes, and settled onto the antique sofa that provided a view out of the parlor's front windows, it was already late afternoon. For the past month, Emily's life had been a hectic cycle of having guests, cleaning rooms, and welcoming new guests. In all that time, she had only had four nights to herself, not counting the resident ghosts.

Those nights had felt absolutely glorious, and she was looking forward to having the next two nights all to herself, too.

Instead of worrying about not making any money on those guest-free nights, Emily was grateful for the physical and mental break. Business was great, and Emily wouldn't have a single quiet night in June or July. Eternal Rest was completely booked for those two months, giving Emily a feeling of both satisfaction and security.

Emily heard the sound of a car rounding the circular driveway, and she stood, stretching her arms up above her head before moving to the front door. She walked onto the front porch, where her best friend, Sage Clark, was already climbing the steps. Sage was wearing a turquoise gauze dress and a giant straw sunhat that completely covered her pink spikes. Her bright-yellow sunglasses completed the ensemble.

Emily snickered. "You going to the beach?"

"I'm happy to search the coast for Scott, if you like," Sage answered airily.

Emily's playful smile faltered. "We've tried so many times, Sage. I don't know how many more failures I can take."

Sage had reached the porch, and she put one hand on Emily's arm. "Hey, don't think of it like that," she said firmly. "Trying to find Scott's spirit somewhere beyond the barrier"—Sage lifted her hand to wave vaguely—"is like trying to find a needle in a haystack. Our past trips haven't been failures. Think of them more as trips to make the haystack smaller."

Emily gave a little shrug. "Except the needle is constantly moving through the haystack, and we don't know in which direction."

Sage narrowed her eyes and gave Emily a long look. "What's going on? You feel strange."

Emily knew Sage was referring to her energy. Having a psychic medium for a best friend was useful, especially since Emily lived in a house filled with ghosts, but sometimes Sage's perceptiveness was uncanny.

There was no point in lying. Sage would see right through that. "Trevor called earlier when I was at the antique store," Emily said. "He offered to come over and help get the things I bought up into the guest rooms, and I refused. He called later, and I refused again, even after I dropped a box full of things down the stairs. I'm not sure where this sudden independent streak is coming from."

"You're still accepting my help," Sage pointed out.

"We've been friends for ages. It's different with you," Emily said.

Sage pursed her lips. "You've proven in the two years since Scott died that you're capable of handling a lot on your own. It's important to remember that just because you can conquer the world all by yourself, it doesn't mean you should. It's good to accept help from time to time."

"As usual, you're absolutely right."

"I know! And I'm here to help you right now. Let's go look for your husband!"

2

Emily flattened the map of Oak Hill on the dining room table. Sage had followed her inside, and both of them were bent over the map. Emily had made little pencil marks in the spots they had already visited. "Let's go up to the lake today," Emily suggested, pointing at a spot northwest of town.

"Good choice," Sage said. "As you already pointed out, I'm dressed for the beach."

Emily folded the map and tucked it into her purse before leading the way out the back door to her car. She didn't need the map—everybody in Oak Hill knew where Lake Otto was—but she still liked having the physical reference point next to her. She and Sage knew from the Eternal Rest ghosts that there was some sort of invisible barrier around Oak Hill that was preventing Scott's spirit from coming home. Why it was there and why Scott was too weak to cross through it even though other ghosts could, were still questions Emily didn't have answers to. At least twice a week for the past month, Emily and Sage had been driving outside of Oak Hill to spots they guessed were beyond the barrier. Sage would attempt to contact Scott, hoping he would somehow sense their presence and come to meet them. So far, the only ghosts Sage had met had been a gold miner, an old couple whose cabin sat in ruins nearby, and a railroad worker. The women had also met swarms of mosquitoes and several foxes.

Sage continued to say encouraging things to Emily during the twenty-minute drive to Lake Otto. Unsurprisingly, the beach was packed with locals taking advantage of the weather. There were also several boats on the water, and as Emily drove along the two-lane road that circled the lake, she spied someone water-skiing.

Emily knew the place she had in mind would be quiet, unlike the beach. The trail that led to the old boathouse was nearly overgrown, and the boathouse itself was little more than wooden piles sticking up out of the shallow water at the edge of the lake. Emily and Scott had discovered the spooky little spot while walking around the lake several years earlier.

Carefully, Emily guided the car off the road and parked in the overgrown grass. She realized as she got out that Sage had actually had the right idea with her attire. The sun beat down, and Emily could already feel the way her T-shirt stuck to her back. She would need another shower when she got home.

As they picked their way along the trail, taking care to avoid the most overgrown areas, Emily felt the temperature begin to dip. The shade of the tall pines above them was offering some respite. "I might want to do this with my feet in the water!" Emily said, turning her head over her shoulder toward Sage.

Emily stopped abruptly when she saw Sage was lagging behind, moving slowly with a nervous look on her face. "Sage?"

"Stop walking," Sage commanded.

Emily complied, looking at her friend curiously. Sage stood still, too, and Emily remained silent, watching as Sage turned her head left to right, slowly. Emily had seen her do that before, when she was trying to channel information from a ghost. Emily liked to think of it as Sage tuning her psychic radio to get a better signal.

Sage's expression didn't change. "Do you feel that?" she asked.

Emily simply shook her head. She watched as Sage either drew in a deep breath or sniffed the air; Emily wasn't quite sure which. Sage's eyes closed for a moment, and Emily found herself leaning forward slightly, listening. She gasped suddenly. "Oh! There aren't any birds!"

"Or bugs," Sage said. "When we got out of the car, you could hear all the life around us, even the buzzing of flies. Now, there's nothing."

Now that she had noticed the silence, too, Emily better understood Sage's hesitance. "What does it mean?" Her voice was barely above a whisper, as if talking in her normal voice might be too disruptive.

"I don't know."

"Do you want to go to a different spot?"

"Yes. No. Yes, but not yet. I want to know what's happening here." Sage's mouth set into a tight line, and she began walking forward again. "Just be on the lookout for anything paranormal."

Emily agreed, hanging back to let Sage take the lead. It was rare for Sage to seem nervous about anything, especially if it had to do with ghosts or other strange activity, but Emily trusted Sage to turn back if she began feeling too uncomfortable.

The crumbling old boathouse looked exactly the same as it had the last time, at least, and Emily felt herself relax as it came into view around a curve in the trail. She was in familiar territory, so even though it looked creepy, it actually felt comforting. A speedboat hummed by beyond the boathouse, and soon tiny tremors in the water reached the shoreline, making a soothing rhythmic sound.

Emily stepped on a rotting board that had once

9

marked the start of the walk from the shore into the boathouse, and the temperature plummeted. She glanced up and saw they were once again in full sunshine, yet it felt like she was standing in front of an open freezer. The cold seemed to be coming from the boathouse, radiating outward.

"Nope," Emily said as she stepped back. Her voice cracked. She knew a sudden cold spot could indicate the presence of a ghost, but this felt different. It wasn't so much a cold spot as it was a vortex of iciness. For a brief moment, Emily had the sensation that it was tugging her forward.

"I know," Sage said. "It didn't feel like this when you were here before?"

"No, not at all. It was a peaceful place. It's like something bad moved in."

"Good girl," Sage said, a note of pride amidst her concern.

Even in a strange situation like this, Emily thought, *she's still trying to teach me to hone my own mediumship skills.*

Sage said firmly, "Let's go. You're not ready for something of this magnitude, and I'm not prepared for it today. We'll find another spot along the lake, one that's not occupied."

Emily didn't need to be told twice. She immediately pivoted and began to walk as quickly as possible, throwing a look over her shoulder every few steps to make sure there wasn't something lurking along the trail behind them.

Once they were inside the car and driving along the road again, Emily glanced at Sage. "Do you know what was causing the cold and that sense of—what's the word —wrongness?"

Sage merely gave a little shrug and kept her eyes forward, apparently too deep in thought to respond.

Emily kept driving until she guessed they were on the

opposite side of the lake from the boathouse. She wanted to be as far away from it as possible. She couldn't see any trail down to the shoreline, but there was a clear spot under the pines next to the side of the road. Sage would just have to commune with the dead while a few cars were passing by.

The heat and humidity felt great after the chill of the boathouse, and Emily happily leaned against the door of her car, her eyes closed and her face turned toward the sky. Behind her eyelids, shadows danced as the pines swayed in a light breeze. "Much better," she said.

"Agreed. Okay, let's get started!"

Emily and Sage found a patch of grass and sat carefully. Sage immediately fell silent and closed her eyes, and Emily knew she was sending out psychic feelers for any ghosts who might be in the area. Hopefully, one of them would be Scott. It was unlikely, but Emily knew they had to keep trying.

It was Kelly Stern, the newest ghost at Eternal Rest, who had alerted Emily to Scott's presence. Kelly had indicated she could see him, just glimpses, really, close to Eternal Rest but unable to actually make it there. When Sage and Emily had first ventured away from Oak Hill in the hopes of getting outside the barrier, they had picked a spot not far from Eternal Rest. Emily had hoped Scott would be there waiting, just on the other side of the barrier. When she was disappointed not to make contact with him on the first try, Sage had reminded her that they knew Scott had traveled as far as Alabama, where he had appeared to a medium in a dream. "The guy gets around, so it might take a while to find him," Sage had quipped. "He's racking up those spiritual frequent flyer miles!"

As they sat in the clearing, Sage's breathing became shallow, and Emily watched her expectantly. She knew she should also be focused, sitting with her eyes closed and her attention on the unseen world around them, but the incident at the boathouse had left her shaken. She felt like someone ought to keep a lookout, even though it was unlikely she would actually see anything paranormal.

As Sage continued to conduct her one-woman séance, Emily glanced at her watch. Sage had been underway for fifteen minutes. As the minutes stretched on, Sage began to murmur, and Emily heard Scott's name among the other words she was saying. Sage's low-pitched, quiet voice blended with the warbles of sparrows perched somewhere nearby and the hum of the breeze flowing through the pines. Emily could feel her eyes growing heavy, and finally she gave in and closed them. Her chin drooped, and she jerked awake when she felt her head tipping forward too far.

Emily blinked. Nothing appeared to have changed in the brief time she had nodded off, yet something was different. Sage was still murmuring, the sun was still shining, and the breeze still blew.

It's the birds. The birds have fallen silent.

Emily felt the briefest bit of panic, but she quickly told herself the birds probably just flew away. She concentrated on the sounds around her, but she heard only the faint hum of a boat engine. She didn't even hear a distant chirp, and no bugs buzzed past.

Sage's eyes snapped open, and Emily knew she had sensed it, too. Without speaking to each other, they both stood and turned to walk the short distance to the car. Emily's hand had just reached the door handle when Sage stopped, letting out a little noise that sounded incredulous and slightly frightened.

"Sage?"

Instead of answering, Sage whirled around to face the clearing. "What do you want? You have thirty seconds before I shut you out, so talk fast!"

Cold air washed over Emily, and she wrapped her arms around herself. Sage began to sway slightly, slowly bringing her hands up, her palms pointed forward and her fingers splayed. "No!" she said firmly. A moment later, she shouted in a commanding tone, "I said no!"

Emily realized she was shaking, not from the cold but from fear. She wanted to grab Sage and pull her into the car, but she was afraid of breaking her friend's concentration. As she watched, she realized the spot at the very center of the clearing was growing dark. It was like the sun had already set on that patch of ground. The spot began to contract, and as it did, it grew darker, more opaque.

Emily thought she could discern arms and legs in the darkness. She had never seen a ghost simply appear like this, despite living and communicating with them regularly. The closest she had gotten was seeing the murdered artist, Robert Gaines, appearing in photos.

Just as Emily moved toward Sage, still not entirely sure what she should do, Sage balled her still-raised hands into fists and brought them down forcefully as she shouted, "No!"

The dark form vanished, and Emily heard a bird chirping.

In front of her, Sage crumpled to the ground.

3

"Sage!" Emily yelled. She rushed forward and knelt down next to her friend.

"I'm all right," Sage mumbled. Slowly, she sat up, keeping her eyes on the spot in the clearing where the form had been. "It's gone. For now."

"What was it? What did it want?" Emily could hear the hysterical edge in her voice.

When Sage spoke again, she sounded stronger. "Let's talk about it somewhere that's not here." She reached a hand toward Emily. "Can you help me up?"

Emily grasped Sage's hand and tugged, and she noted how gingerly Sage was moving. "Are you hurt?" she asked.

"Just exhausted. That was intense."

Sage didn't say anything else until they were several miles away from the lake. Emily knew she was speeding, but she didn't care. She kept her eyes on the road ahead as Sage began, "I haven't felt anything like that in years. Not since college."

"What was it? At first, I thought it was a ghost, but it seemed like something… darker."

"I don't know what it was. It could have been a ghost— a really angry one, at that. The couple of times I've sensed an entity like that, I've shut down communication immediately. I don't want to open myself up to dark energies."

"Then why did you give this one a chance to communicate?"

"It followed us from the boathouse, Em. It either followed your car or sensed us over on the other side of the lake. I figured if it was working that hard, then maybe it had something important to say."

Emily glanced in her rearview mirror, almost expecting to see a dark shadow flying down the road behind them. "Is it following us now?"

"I think we're safe. It took everything I had to cut myself off from it psychically. Its presence felt invasive."

"I'm sorry, Sage. This wouldn't have happened if we weren't out here looking for Scott." Even amid her fear, Emily could also feel her disappointment that yet another scouting trip had been for nothing.

Sage actually gave a little laugh. "Don't be sorry. I want to help Scott, too. And remember, I'm the one who let the entity establish a line of contact."

"I wonder what it really wanted?"

"Nothing good."

"If it wasn't a ghost, then what was it?"

"I don't know, Em."

The rest of the drive was silent. When they reached Eternal Rest, Emily hugged Sage tightly while both thanking her and apologizing again. Sage just gave her a squeeze and said, "I'll be fine after a good night's sleep. I think you'll be perfectly safe tonight, but you call me if anything strange happens." Sage released Emily and stepped back, giving her a stern look. "And I mean anything."

"I will. And I'll ask the ghosts to be on the lookout."

Emily stood on her front porch and watched Sage drive away. Before going inside the house, Emily sat on the porch swing for a few minutes, enjoying the sound of birds in a nearby oak tree. She took the chirping as reassurance that the entity hadn't followed her home. To Emily's left, several people were coming out of historic Hilltop Cemetery. She gave them a little wave and watched as they walked to a van in the grassy parking area next to the road.

Once she went inside, Emily sank down onto the parlor sofa. She felt the irony of sitting in the same spot where she had been before the excursion to the lake. It was almost like it hadn't really happened. *I may as well have stayed right here.* The thought gave Emily an idea, and she sat up, suddenly feeling excited.

"Mrs. Thompson? Kelly? Grandma Gray?" Emily called loudly.

A few moments later, Emily heard two sounds at once: both a knock on the wall and the sound of something landing on the floor behind her. The knock, she knew, was the ghost of Mrs. Thompson rapping on the wall to acknowledge her presence. Emily stood and walked toward her desk, where the other sound had come from. She wasn't surprised to see a pencil lying on the floor. Her eyes went right to the sheet of paper next to her laptop. Kelly had written *hey* in her usual big, swooping letters. Grandma Gray, or GG for short, wasn't typically as communicative as the other two, so Emily simply hoped she was there, too. She bent down to retrieve the pencil and put it in its regular spot on the rolltop desk.

"Ladies, I have a big favor to ask," Emily began. "You know I'm trying to find Scott's spirit so I can help him cross over and find peace, but he seems to be stuck outside this mysterious psychic barrier around Oak Hill. Sage and I have been trying to go outside the barrier to look for him, but I can't be gone from the house for long if I have guests, and, of course, we can't cover a lot of ground. I bet you ghosts could go a lot farther, a lot faster. Am I right?"

Mrs. Thompson knocked in affirmation. Emily smiled, thinking how much the elderly woman must enjoy being able to zoom around now that she was deceased. *No more arthritis pain for her.*

"Would you three be willing to go look for Scott? Kelly, you've seen him on the other side of the barrier, and Mrs. Thompson knew Scott in life, so you two can let GG know who to look for."

Knowing Kelly wouldn't write a message if Emily were watching, she walked to the front of the room and looked through one of the floor-to-ceiling windows overlooking the front yard. The sun was still above the tree line, even though it was nearly dinnertime.

After waiting for what she hoped was long enough for Kelly to respond, Emily returned to her desk. Kelly had written *yes, yes, yes* with five exclamation points and a smiley face. Sometimes, it was easy for Emily to simply think of Kelly as a ghost, and not as the energetic teenager she had been in life. Responses like this reminded her that Kelly had only been seventeen when she was killed.

"Thanks, Kelly. Mrs. Thompson, what about you? Are you willing to go on a little road trip?"

Mrs. Thompson knocked so hard, the painting of Eternal Rest Emily had recently hung above her desk vibrated against the wall.

"And GG will go, too?" Emily asked.

Knock.

Emily grinned, wondering why she hadn't thought of this before. It made so much more sense to send ghosts to seek one of their own. "Thanks, you three. If—no, *when* you find Scott, tell him we want to help him. Ask him what we need to do. And be safe. There are some nasty spirits out there."

There was no need for her ghosts to grab purses or put on shoes before heading out the door. They would just go, Emily knew. She trusted they had done just that as she went to the kitchen to make dinner for herself. It wasn't until she was sitting at the small wooden table in the corner of the kitchen, halfway through a bowl of spaghetti, that Emily realized how very alone she felt. She stopped eating and put her fork down, sitting back to gaze around the kitchen.

Emily had only recently begun developing her skills as a psychic medium, urged on by Sage. Until about two months before, Emily would have laughed if anyone had suggested she might have some kind of sixth sense. She had never felt like she possessed any kind of abilities, and yet, at that moment, she realized how different the house felt without her ghosts.

It wasn't that the house was more quiet with the ghosts gone, Emily realized. She occasionally heard footsteps upstairs, and of course, Mrs. Thompson liked to knock, but usually only when Emily or Sage asked her to. Instead, what Emily was feeling was more like a sense of loneliness. Ghosts might be able to turn the air around them cold, but without her own ghosts at home, Eternal Rest didn't feel as warm.

Not only did she feel lonely, but Emily also felt isolated. After being followed by the entity at the lake, Emily was especially cognizant of how separated she was from the rest of the world. Eternal Rest was outside the more developed area of Oak Hill, without any close neighbors except the thousands of dead buried at the cemetery next door.

The second her thoughts started going in that direction, Emily called her mom, hoping the chat would distract her. Getting an earful of the latest Oak Hill gossip did the trick, and later, Emily went to bed thinking not about ghosts but the rumor that a new barbecue restaurant would be opening on the square downtown.

Emily only woke up one time during the night. She had been a light sleeper since Scott's fatal car crash two years before, but with no guests and no ghosts, the silence of Eternal Rest had allowed Emily to sleep well. She had woken up sometime around five o'clock in the morning, thinking she had heard a shout. She had sat straight up in bed and fumbled for the switch on the nightstand lamp, but even before her eyes adjusted to the sudden brightness, she was already telling herself it was nothing. She had been caught between dreaming and waking, and surely the shouting was coming from a dream.

In fact, she had told herself, *I was probably having a night-mare that I had a disgruntled guest, and he was yelling at me.*

In the morning, Emily sipped coffee, responded to emails, and confirmed some reservation requests for the fall. In between her tasks, she wondered idly what the word was for a house that used to have ghosts but didn't anymore. If ghosts arrived at a place, it was said to be haunted. So would that mean Eternal Rest was now unhaunted? Hauntless? Whatever the right way to phrase it might be, it didn't change the fact that the atmosphere in the house still felt decidedly different.

The morning seemed to pass slowly as Emily resigned herself to taking care of a few things on her to-do list that she had been avoiding. It was easy not to feel obligated to do them when she had lots of guests and rooms that constantly needed to be cleaned, but today she had plenty of time and no more ready excuses.

Emily was wrapping up a fight with tendrils of ivy that were trying to snake their way up the dark-blue clapboard at the rear of the house when she realized it was nearly time for lunch. She was sweaty from pulling down the ivy, not to mention dirty despite the gardening gloves she was wearing, and she would have just enough time for a quick shower.

It was one o'clock exactly as Emily pulled into the parking lot of This is a Stickup, a quirky restaurant housed inside an old bank. The menu featured skewers of meat and vegetables that had been cooked on a grill, and they were served on special trays designed so the skewers stuck straight up. Emily had always felt like the pun was a bit of a stretch, but she had to admit the food was good.

Trevor was already seated at a table in a back corner when Emily went in. He was looking around the room, and Emily knew he was soaking in the mug shots of famous bank robbers and old wanted posters that adorned the walls. "It's kitschy but fun," she said as she slid into the chair opposite Trevor.

"Is it haunted?" His bright-blue eyes left the walls and looked at Emily excitedly.

"That's a good question. We'll have to ask! But first, thanks for the recommendation on that local winery. My guests at the last Spirited Saturday Night absolutely loved their chardonnay."

"I still can't believe you'd never heard of the place," Trevor answered. His expression was teasing as he added, "Sometimes, I don't think you get out enough. You're like a hermit out there in your haunted house."

"I definitely don't get out enough!"

"The next time you have a day off, let's go to the winery for a tasting."

"So, sometime in September, maybe."

"Oh, right. I keep forgetting you've got a packed house all summer. When are you going to get another assistant?"

Emily threw her hands up in mock exasperation. "It's not for lack of trying on my part! I've had two in the past month. Two, Trevor. The first one heard footsteps upstairs while he was alone in the house and quit right then, and the other had to leave town to go take care of a sick relative."

Trevor was nodding. "I knew about the spooked assistant, but I didn't realize there had been another one who's come and gone already."

"Maybe Mrs. Thompson put a curse on the position." Emily was trying to joke, but a part of her felt like it might actually be true. Mrs. Thompson had been a wonderful assistant, but ever since she died and took up residence at Eternal Rest as a ghost, Emily just couldn't keep the position filled.

A server came to take their drink order, and as soon as he was gone, Emily snapped open her menu. "I'm starving," she said, intentionally steering the conversation away from ghosts. Talking about them only reminded her she'd be going home to an empty house after lunch. "I worked hard this morning."

It wasn't until after they had gotten their drinks and ordered food that Emily suddenly realized Trevor was unusually quiet. She put down her glass of sweet tea and gazed at him, noticing for the first time how worn out he looked. "What's wrong?" she asked.

Trevor gave her a small smile. "Is your intuition kicking in, or do I look that bad?"

"You look tired, that's all. And you're not chatting as much as usual."

"It's my dad," he said quietly. "He's dying."

Trevor took a deep breath and ran a hand through his thick dark hair. "Sorry to drop that bombshell on you," he mumbled, his eyes lowering to the table.

"I'm so sorry, Trevor," Emily said with feeling. She knew Trevor's relationship with his dad was strained—after all, his dad was a convicted murderer—but his battle with cancer was the reason Trevor had moved back to Oak Hill in the first place. "Have you seen him recently?"

"I saw him last week, and I'm going over to the jail again after we eat. He seemed to rebound a bit after—you know—but he's really taken a turn for the worse. He's been saying all along that he didn't expect to make it to the end of this year, but it's still hard to take."

Emily reached forward and put her hand over Trevor's. The "you know" had been a reference to her figuring out that Mr. Williams had killed Kelly Stern, right in the middle of Hilltop Cemetery. Since he had also tried to kill his own two sons, Emily didn't feel a lot of sympathy for him. She did, however, feel sympathy for Trevor. Knowing she needed to say something comforting, she finally managed, "It's good that you came back to town to spend time with him. I'm sure he appreciates having you here."

"He asked about you last week."

"Oh?"

"Yeah. He wanted to know, and this is a direct quote, if 'that nosy widowed girl' was still in my life." Trevor shook his head and gave an incredulous laugh. "I told him you were, and that after lots of rescheduling, we had finally met up for coffee. I skipped telling him about helping you solve a murder at the arts festival. That subject matter seemed to hit a little too close to home."

Emily patted Trevor's hand, then leaned back again. "If 'nosy' is the worst word he can think of to call me, then I consider myself very lucky." After a pause, Emily asked shyly, "So, what happens once you don't need to be here for him anymore? Will you move back to Atlanta?"

Trevor's eyebrows drew together, and he looked at Emily thoughtfully. "Honestly, I don't know. I'm enjoying being back in Oak Hill, but I don't know if I want to stay at the design firm here long-term. I don't even know if I want to be a graphic designer for the rest of my life."

"What else would you like to do?"

Trevor still looked introspective as he answered, "Well, helping catch killers seems like a pretty fulfilling career path."

Emily wasn't sure if Trevor was being serious or just teasing. "Are you planning to be the newest detective with the Oak Hill Police Department?"

"I don't know." Trevor smiled suddenly, the creases in his forehead disappearing to make him look younger. "There's no need to make any decisions just yet. Right now, I want to know when I can come check out the newest antiques at Eternal Rest. I hear a lot of effort went into getting them into the house."

Emily balled up her napkin and threw it squarely at Trevor's face.

After lunch, Emily ran a few errands around Oak Hill before heading back to Eternal Rest. She had felt energized after her lunch with Trevor, enjoying his company and the satisfaction of feeling like she was a help to him, giving him a much-needed break from focusing on his father's health.

It was mid-afternoon by the time Emily tottered up the back steps, a grocery bag balanced in each arm. She rolled her eyes at her own stubbornness. "What would Trevor say?" she asked herself. His teasing at lunch was still fresh in her mind. She put the bags down, unlocked the door, and took the bags into the kitchen one at a time. It had been bad enough dropping the box of antiques, and the last thing she wanted to do was send a bottle of wine crashing to the floor.

Once the groceries were put away, Emily reluctantly turned to her to-do list. She had been putting off organizing the attic for far too long. It had once been so tidy, with Christmas and Halloween decorations stacked neatly in their plastic bins and old pieces of art and furniture carefully leaned against the walls. Now, the gabled room up on the third story looked like a jumbled mess.

Emily put on shorts and an old T-shirt, grabbed her bucket of cleaning supplies from the cabinet under the kitchen sink, and headed upstairs. The staircase that led from the ground-floor hallway up to the guest rooms was wide and pretty, with a carved banister that swooped gracefully on each end. The staircase to the attic was steep and narrow, and it usually stayed hidden behind a door at the back of the second floor.

Emily had loved the hidden staircase as a child, back when her grandparents still owned Eternal Rest. She had enjoyed clambering up it to the play and nap area that had been set up in the attic for her and her cousins, and she had always felt like an explorer discovering parts of the house that guests would never get to see. As an adult, Emily simply found the stairs cramped and annoying.

The attic, though, was still a place of wonder to Emily. The ceiling sloped down on each side, and the single light fixture hanging from the center of the room barely illuminated the low-hung corners. Emily often discovered things in those shadowy areas that she hadn't seen since childhood, and on rare occasions, she would find something entirely new to her. Several pieces of art now hanging in the guest rooms had been found squeezed between an old steamer trunk and the wall.

The plastic storage bins full of Halloween decorations were neatly stacked, but the Christmas bins were a disaster. Emily had been busy after the holiday season, and many items hadn't been properly put away. There were little piles of things—stockings, strings of lights, and garland among them—scattered throughout the attic. Several bins were overflowing, their lids thrown aside.

Emily sidestepped the mess to turn on a beat-up radio, which sat on an old, scratched dresser. Once music from the local rock station was blaring from the radio, she got to work.

It wasn't long before Emily had the Christmas items back in their proper places. She sighed in satisfaction as she stepped back to admire the neat stack of bins, then shook her head when she realized she would be pulling all those items out again in just six months.

With the worst part of the job done, Emily retrieved her feather duster from the cleaning bucket and began working her way through the attic. She moved in time to the beat of the song playing, dancing just as much as dusting.

The song ended, and in the brief silence before the

deejay began to introduce the next song, Emily heard a shout. She frowned in the direction of the radio, initially assuming someone at the station must have been shouting.

That sure sounded like the shout that woke me up last night.

That thought was quickly followed by another: *But that was just a dream. Wasn't it?*

Emily suddenly felt chilled, even though it was always too warm in the attic during the summer months. The feather duster hung limp at her side as she walked quickly to the radio and turned it off. She listened as she pictured the layout of the house below her feet.

Silence.

As Emily felt her sense of calm returning, she shook her head and turned on the radio again, telling herself firmly it had just been someone shouting at the radio station, their voice loud enough for the microphone to pick it up. Nevertheless, she finished her cleaning quickly, no longer dancing to the music but working efficiently. She didn't hear any more shouting, but she still felt a sense of relief when she was once again in the more-familiar kitchen.

Emily cleaned up, poured a big glass of sweet tea, and went to her desk in the parlor. She had mostly shaken the feeling of being spooked, but she still felt slightly uncom-fortable. She scrolled through several emails before finally giving up and sitting back, her eyes moving up to the painting of Eternal Rest.

The only explanation Emily could come up with for her strange feeling was the fact that her house was devoid of its ghosts. She could still feel their absence, almost like its own kind of unseen presence. Emily was also keenly aware of the fact that her ghosts had always been an easy excuse for anything unusual that happened. Items went missing, strange noises, eerie feelings of not being alone, all could be attributed to the ghosts. And, since the ghosts of Eternal Rest were friendly, there was nothing scary about those occurrences. If Emily suddenly heard the flush of an upstairs toilet, even when she had no guests, she would just smile and tell herself Mrs. Thompson must be up there tidying the bathroom.

Now, knowing her ghosts were out searching for Scott, Emily didn't have a ready excuse for anything strange that happened. One shout had been in her mind, and the other had come from the radio. The fact that both noises had sounded so similar was just a coincidence. At least, that was what Emily was telling herself.

Three loud knocks sounded, and Emily nearly jumped out of her chair. She gasped, wondering what else was haunting her home. Mrs. Thompson was the one who communicated with knocking, but she wasn't there. Had the entity from the lake followed her home, after all? Had a ghost from the cemetery noticed there were vacancies at Eternal Rest and moved in?

Emily's heart was pounding, but when she heard the three knocks a second time, she mumbled, "I am so silly."

It was just someone at the door. *Of course, it's just the door,* Emily told herself as she got up. *It can't be a ghost, because there are no ghosts here.*

Emily was surprised when she opened the door and saw her friend Trish Alden standing there. It was the right time for Trish to make her usual delivery—almost six o'clock—but Emily hadn't put in an order for Grainy Day Bakery goods since she didn't have any guests.

Trish had taken her long blonde hair out of its usual French braid, and it fell in chunky waves over her shoulders. "Hey, Emily!" Trish said in her thick Southern accent. "You still looking for an assistant?"

"I am. And hi to you, too."

"I've got great news! My Aunt Mona is moving back to Oak Hill. She's retiring from teaching down in Dublin, and when she told me she'd want to find some part-time work, I told her I had the perfect job for her. I hope you don't mind! She's smart, she's really good with people, and she's cool with ghosts!"

Emily grinned. "Trish, thank you! She sounds like a great fit! When would she be available to start?"

"She'll be here at the end of July."

Emily's smile faltered. That was more than two months away and after the busy season when she would most need help. "Oh. Well, I really need someone for June and July, too."

"Oh, I've also got that figured out for you. Once Clint wraps up school for the year, he can come work for you over the summer. He's saving up to buy himself a car. He's already helping me at the bakery after school, but I don't think he wants to work for his mama all day, every day. If he can work for you a couple days a week, then help me as needed at the bakery, everyone wins."

Now Emily's smile was back in full force. Clint was just a teenager, but Trish and her husband had raised him to be a polite, even-tempered kid. He would be a great assistant, especially since he was strong enough to haul any future antique purchases up the stairs without breaking a sweat.

Emily agreed to Trish's proposal enthusiastically, promising to talk with her in more detail soon, then wished her a good night. It wasn't until Emily had watched Trish pull her car onto the road that she started to laugh. She couldn't remember the last time Trish had stopped by without giving her a single piece of Oak Hill gossip.

Still smiling, Emily shut the front door and turned toward the parlor. She had just taken her first step when she heard a screeching noise, like fingernails dragging across a chalkboard.

Emily clamped her hands over her ears and shrank against the front door. This time, she couldn't explain away the strange noise.

5

It was the muscles in Emily's lower back that eventually forced her to stand up straight and think rationally. She had finally moved her hands, but she had stayed crouched in front of the door as she anticipated another disruption.

Emily couldn't imagine what had made the horrible noise, but it was far worse than the shouting. It was less human, and the sound physically hurt her ears. As she finally stood, her muscles protesting the tense, cramped position they had been in, Emily chided herself. She had faced down ghosts in other places without feeling this kind of fear, so why was she acting like this now?

Because this is my home. The answer was so obvious. It was one thing to go to a different place, like the crumbling Mountain View Manor outside of town, and encounter ghosts, but this was Emily's home, her escape from the rest of the world.

Except, if something new had taken up residence at Eternal Rest, then her home was no longer the safe refuge it had once been.

In that moment, Emily realized her fear wasn't just because her home possibly had a new haunting. She was also worried it wasn't simply a ghost looking for a home but that thing from the lake.

30

In a flash, Emily was outside on her porch, her cell phone raised to her ear.

Sage picked up on the second ring. "What's up, Em?"

"I think it followed me home." Emily didn't bother to elaborate further. She knew Sage understood.

"Have you seen it?"

"No, but I've heard a couple of weird things today, and it can't be my ghosts, because I asked them to go look for Scott."

"Oh, clever idea! We'll talk about that later. Do you feel that intense cold like we felt at the lake?"

"No."

"Do you feel like you're in danger?"

Emily paused before answering, trying to assess her own feelings. Two shouts and the nails-on-chalkboard sound didn't really count as threats, she decided. She also took a moment to do exactly what Sage would have requested: she tried tuning in to her intuition. Finally, she said, "My gut says I'm not in danger. I think I'm scared because I'm worried it might be that thing, but, ultimately, I don't feel like I'm being actively threatened."

"I think your gut is right," Sage said reassuringly. "But just in case, want me to come over?"

Emily glanced to her left and saw a form walking under the arched iron gateway of the cemetery. Even in the gathering shadows, she recognized Reed Marshall. "Actually, Reed is leaving Hilltop right now. I'll ask him to come over."

Sage's tone turned teasing as she responded, "But I thought you were going through an independent streak and didn't want anyone's help?"

Emily groaned. "It's Reed, and I'm asking for help with a haunting, not help hauling boxes. That's different. Plus, I think he knows more than he lets on about ghostly matters. He'll have some wisdom for me, I'm sure."

"Of course he will, but call if you need me, okay?"

Emily was already walking down the porch steps and waving toward the cemetery as she said goodbye to Sage. After locking the cemetery gate, Reed had taken the well-tended path that arced left toward the roadside parking lot. When he saw Emily waving, he steered right to take the dirt path that connected Eternal Rest and Hilltop Cemetery.

As he got closer, Reed raised a hand and called, "Good evening, Emily!"

"You're working late tonight," Emily noted.

"I stayed late to do some gardening at my family's plot." Reed took a lot of pride in his work as a sexton, and he took even more pride in maintaining the old Marshall family plot. When he reached Emily, Reed stopped and peered at her with his dark-brown eyes. "Something happened."

"Seriously, when are you going to admit that your cousin isn't the only one who inherited the family gift?"

"I make no claims of being psychic." One corner of Reed's mouth lifted, and it only made Emily doubt his denial even more. "Is this something we need to discuss over a glass of wine?"

"I'll pour you a glass, but none for me."

"Oh." Reed's expression turned serious. "It's that bad."

Emily held up a hand. "I'm okay, and I don't think I'm in danger, but it's been an unsettling couple of days. If you have time, I'd love some advice."

Soon, Emily and Reed were seated at the table in the kitchen. Reed had a glass of wine in his hand, and Emily was slowly twirling a glass of sweet tea sitting in front of her. She mostly kept her eyes focused on the ice cubes bobbing in the glass while she spoke, telling Reed every-thing she and Sage had experienced at the lake, as well as her concerns about the current activity in the house.

Reed remained silent the whole time, allowing Emily to simply get it all out in the open. When she finished talking and finally raised her eyes to his, he put down his glass and said calmly, "I think Sage is right. You don't need to be worried about whatever new entity might be hanging out here."

"What makes you say that?"

Reed sat back and gestured around the room. "Your house, Emily, it has a personality. When I come here, I can feel how warm and happy this place is. I don't know what the house felt like before your grandparents bought it, but they poured so much love into restoring it and making it a welcoming place for guests. You and Scott carried on that effort when you took over for them. Even when Kelly's ghost first showed up and was so scared and angry, the house still felt good. It still feels that way now. While your new visitor might not be all sunshine and rainbows, I don't think they're evil, either."

"That's the impression I'm getting, too, but it's comforting to hear you say it," Emily said with feeling. "And the word 'evil' seems like the right choice for that thing at the lake."

Reed actually chuckled. "When you call it 'that thing at the lake,' all I can think of is some kind of green, slimy lake monster."

"I think that would have been less scary! I've never felt something so dark before."

Reed turned serious again. "You've been lucky. My great-aunt had some stories, and I know my cousin has had to psychically fend off dark entities before. There are bad things in the spirit world, just as there are bad people in the living world."

"Oak Hill seems to have fairly friendly ghosts. Not dangerous ones, at least."

"You're right," Reed said slowly. "Now that I think of

it, I can't recall a single story about a truly evil haunting in this town."

"Good point. I knew you'd make me feel better!" Emily finally lifted her glass and took a drink. As she set her glass down, she heard more than just the thunk of the glass against the wood. There was a quiet, high-pitched noise at the same time. "There it is! Did you hear that?"

It was obvious Reed had, in fact, heard the sound. He was sitting up straight, his head turned toward the kitchen door. "I think it's coming from upstairs," he said quietly. He rose slowly, barely making any sound. "Let's go see what we find!"

Emily tiptoed up the stairs behind Reed, following his lead in being as quiet as possible so they could hear the sound if it happened again. On the landing, Reed stopped abruptly, and Emily walked right into him. "Sorry!" she mouthed. She backed up but kept one hand on Reed's arm, deciding that even if she didn't have anything to be scared of, she was still more comfortable keeping him close.

The two of them stood there on the landing, barely moving, for five minutes. Neither one of them heard a sound, except for the thunk and hum of the air conditioner turning on. Finally, Emily called, "Hello? Can you please make that noise again?" Her voice felt loud after the long silence, and she could hear the false cheer in it.

Still, there was nothing.

"It could have been something outside, like a branch against a window pane," Reed suggested. Emily could hear the doubt in his voice.

"Yeah. Let's wait a couple more minutes, just in case."

They waited longer than that, long enough that Emily finally released Reed's arm and leaned against the wall, one ankle crossed over the other. It was Emily who finally called a halt to the informal ghost hunt. "Let's go back downstairs. You're right, Reed. I'm so used to ghosts and their activity that I hear a noise and instantly assume it's paranormal. It could absolutely be something totally normal."

"You've forgotten how to be a skeptic."

"Sage wants me to dive in to explore my abilities, and I need to find the balance between reaching out to that world and being rational."

"Just remember that the next time something unusual happens."

Emily offered to cook Reed dinner, and he happily accepted. While she cooked, Emily plied Reed with questions about Kat Mason, the artist he'd gone out with a few times during the recent arts festival. Reed was vague in his answers, saying only that Kat was doing well and that she was currently at a festival in New York. Emily glanced away from the stove just in time to catch the satisfied little smile on Reed's face. She turned back to the pan of simmering sauce, biting her lip to keep from teasing him. Reed had been a friend for a long time, and lately he was becoming more like a big brother. She was happy he and Kat had something together. Emily allowed herself only a few seconds of self-pity. *If I wanted to date someone, I'm sure I could,* she told herself resolutely.

By the time Reed left, Emily was yawning. It had been a long but productive day, and she flopped into bed, turned off the light, and fell asleep within two minutes.

This time, the nightstand clock read two thirty-four when Emily woke to what sounded like distant shouting. Again, she blinked and listened, wondering if she had really heard something, or if she had woken up at the tail end of a dream. Reed's words came floating back into her mind, his gentle reminder that not everything strange that happened had to be paranormal. Dreams could be bizarre, but that space between dreaming and waking could be even more disorienting. The shouting could have been a dream, and Emily reminded herself that even the shouting she had heard in the attic could have come from the radio.

Besides, Emily assured herself, she still didn't feel like she was in danger. She eventually fell back to sleep, though she left the nightstand lamp on.

When Emily woke up again, this time with her alarm clock announcing it was time to get up, she got out of bed reluctantly. As she shuffled to the kitchen to turn on the coffee maker, she realized she didn't feel refreshed. She only remembered waking up the one time during the night, but she still felt sluggish.

Emily spent the morning alternating between drinking coffee and fielding phone calls. Now that Eternal Rest was so popular, she hated having to tell so many people that the dates they wanted to book were sold out. She could hear the disappointment in their voices. Some people were happy to choose other dates, though, and Emily was already booking rooms as far out as February of the following year.

Emily had just gotten off the phone with someone wondering if they could book two rooms over New Year's when her doorbell rang. Her guests for the week had arrived.

6

Emily opened the door to see five eager faces beaming at her. "Hi!" said the young woman standing at the front of the group. "I know we're a little early, but we didn't have as much traffic as we expected in Atlanta. We thought we'd at least come by to see if we can leave our luggage here before we go explore Oak Hill. Oh, my gosh, I'm just so excited to finally be here!"

"Welcome to Eternal Rest," Emily answered, stepping back to wave the group in. "You're only an hour early, so you can go ahead and check in. Your rooms are ready."

The group moved in a tight knot as Emily directed them toward the parlor. Once they were seated on the sofa and the wingback chairs, Emily stood between the windows to address them. "So, any special requests for which rooms you're in? You five have the place to yourselves this week, so you can choose the rooms you want."

The woman who had first spoken raised her hand. "I want to stay in Jaxon Knight-MacGinn's room!" She practically shouted the request in her excitement.

"Oh, you've been reading up on our recent, ah, adventures," Emily said, feeling a little flustered. She had been expecting ghost hunters, not true crime enthusiasts.

"Yes, of course. I mean, we had booked this stay before that happened, but maybe his ghost is still here, and we can communicate with him!" The woman's cheeks were flushed, and her blue eyes were wide as she, apparently, imagined the conversations she would have with Jaxon's ghost.

"I'm sorry to say, he's not here anymore. He crossed over." Emily paused, then added, "Actually, I'm not that sorry. He was a jerk, even as a ghost. I do *not* miss him."

The woman's face fell, but the other four guests laughed amiably.

Emily moved to her desk to retrieve room keys, then walked straight to the woman, who was again looking excited. "Here's the key to room one. Jaxon's room. It's right above the parlor here. What's your name?"

"Catherine Simms. It'll be me and my boyfriend, Blake Newman, in that room." Catherine jerked her chin toward the tall, thin man sitting to her right, her long, blonde hair swinging with the movement. Blake's shoulders were rolled forward, and his brown eyes were focused on his folded hands.

"Hi," he said softly, looking up at Emily only briefly.

One of the other men in the group spoke up, clearly more outgoing than Blake. "I'm Hal Henderson. I'd love a room with a view of the cemetery, please."

Emily handed him a key, explaining that room three was just behind Catherine and Blake's, and it afforded a clear view of Hilltop Cemetery. Hal rose, and Emily noticed how fit he was under his khaki pants and white polo shirt. Combined with his tan and sun-bleached hair, he looked more like he should be at a yacht club than at a haunted bed and breakfast in North Georgia.

The other two guests, another couple, introduced themselves as Andy and Annie. "We know," Annie said, raising her hands defensively, even though she was smiling playfully. Her light-brown wavy hair shone in the sunlight coming through the windows. "It sounds made up, like we should be a company selling fancy, overpriced throw pillows or something."

"And we don't care which room we're in," Andy added. Emily noticed how similar he looked to Hal, except his hair hung below his shoulders. She raised an eyebrow, looking from one to the other. Andy nodded and smiled. "Yeah, we're brothers. I dragged Hal into this whole ghost hunting thing."

"Kicking and screaming," Hal agreed.

"And now he's the best at getting EVPs," Catherine piped up. "It's like ghosts are just dying to talk to him"— she stopped and snickered at her play on words—"and they leave messages on his tape recorder all the time."

Emily nodded in appreciation. "That's a valuable trait for a paranormal investigator. Andy and Annie, you two will be above the dining room." Emily pointed toward the other side of the hall. "The room faces the front yard, so it's a nice view of the Blue Ridge Mountains on the horizon."

As her guests rose to get settled into their rooms, Emily invited them to come back down for sweet tea when they were ready. Hal politely requested unsweetened before Emily made her way to the kitchen.

Twenty minutes later, Emily once again stood before her guests in the parlor, passing out glasses of iced tea. After a few quiet moments as the five guests took their first sips, Catherine put her glass down on the coffee table and looked at Emily expectantly. "So, tell us about the ghosts here, and how to best communicate with them!"

It was only then that Emily realized her mistake, and she dropped her head into her hands. "Oh, no," she groaned.

She could practically feel her guests' confusion, and taking a deep breath, she relaxed her hands and looked up.

"I'm so, so sorry," she began, "but Eternal Rest isn't haunted right now."

Five blank faces stared up at her.

"What do you mean?" Catherine asked. "How can a haunted place not be haunted anymore?"

"She didn't say 'anymore,'" Andy pointed out. "She said it's not haunted 'right now,' which implies the ghosts are on vacation."

"Or on strike," Annie piped up with a little giggle.

"I... sent them on an errand," Emily said. She was mentally kicking herself for being so stupid. She had been so excited at the idea of having her ghosts look for Scott that she had simply sent them off without stopping to consider the possible consequences. Eternal Rest was popular largely because of its reputation as haunted, and paranormal investigation teams like this one were a huge part of her business. Emily thought hard, looking for some consolation for her guests, and came up with, "However, there is the ghost of a child still here. They don't show up often, but I do have some toys you can ask them to play with. And, of course, the cemetery is haunted, too."

"What kind of an errand?" Blake asked. He was sitting up straighter now and looking much more interested in the scene around him.

Emily gestured in the direction of the cemetery. She was planning to give Blake a simple answer, but instead, she said, "There's a psychic barrier around this town, and the spirit of my late husband is trapped somewhere outside of it. He needs help, and so I've asked my ghosts to go look for him. I'm sorry. I will gladly give you a discount for your stay, and you can come back in the future, once they've returned." She stopped, realizing she was out of breath. In her anxiousness about disappointing her guests, she was speaking quickly, her breathing shallow.

Catherine looked like she was on the verge of

complaining. She crossed her arms over her chest and pushed herself against the back of the sofa with a huff. Blake, though, was leaning forward. "How can we help?" he asked.

The question caught Emily off guard, and she stammered before managing to say, "I don't know if you can. Scott is weak, which is why he can't get through the barrier. We don't know why the barrier is there or who made it. Right now, it's up to my ghosts to find him."

Blake started chewing on a fingernail absently. "We can ask the ghosts at the cemetery about this barrier. This sounds really interesting."

Hal and Annie both nodded, and Andy said, "We need to make the most of the next three nights if we're going to help Emily."

Emily could only smile in gratitude, even though she doubted the ghost hunters would be able to actually accomplish anything for Scott. Still, if they were going to view this as motivation, rather than being upset about the absence of her most active ghosts, then she was thankful.

Emily's guests left for downtown Oak Hill shortly after their discussion wrapped up. They were hungry after the morning's drive up from Jacksonville, so Emily gave them directions to The Depot, making them promise to say hello to the owner, Jay, for her.

By the time the group returned to Eternal Rest, dark clouds were gathering on the western horizon, and the breeze was picking up. Andy and Annie came into the parlor, where Emily was sitting at her desk. "It's not looking good for us to visit the cemetery tonight," Andy said. "It's supposed to be rainy all night."

Emily swiveled around in her chair so she could face

them. "Hilltop's ghosts will still be there tomorrow. Maybe you can try to communicate with the child here in the house tonight."

"That's what we were just discussing. Can you please get those toys you mentioned? We'll get our equipment set up now, so we'll be ready to go as soon as it gets dark."

Emily retrieved a ball, a little wooden horse on wheels, and a set of blocks from the attic. She hadn't had any requests for the toys in a long time, and she was glad to have noticed them in one corner of the attic when she had been cleaning.

For the remainder of the afternoon, Emily's guests set up video cameras in the guest rooms and dining room. They put a large monitor in the kitchen—which was the usual spot for teams to use as a base of operations during an investigation—that would show each camera's feed. Emily hated that they were going to so much effort for a ghost that was unreliable. Even Sage hadn't been able to glean any information from the ghostly child.

Outside, the sky continued to grow darker as the storm clouds rolled in and the sun sank behind them. Forks of lightning shot across the horizon, and Emily finally gave up working to go stand in the open front doorway—she could have a nice view of the light show without feeling exposed to its dangers.

Emily heard footsteps behind her and turned to see Hal. "You know," she said offhandedly, "lightning is supposed to enhance paranormal activity. My best friend taught me that. It's extra energy for the ghosts to harness."

Hal nodded. "That makes sense. I just got into this stuff about a year ago. Andy kept pestering me to join them, and I finally gave in. I got an EVP on my first investigation of a little girl asking for her mommy. It was eerie, but I was hooked."

"What's your group's name?"

"First Coast Ghost Hunters." Hal grinned. "Say that five times fast! Jacksonville doesn't have a ton of ghosts, but St. Augustine is nearby, and it's crawling with spirits. We get to investigate a lot of cool old places."

"I'd love to go to St. Augustine someday!"

Emily heard thumping feet on the stairs, and soon she heard Catherine's voice saying, "Let's get started! There's no reason to wait until it's late at night. We can investigate for a couple of hours, then take a dinner break."

"Won't the sound of the rain interfere with EVPs?" Hal asked.

"It won't be so loud once the door is closed. Let's go!" Without waiting for an answer, Catherine turned and bounded down the hallway.

Soon, Emily's guests were huddled in the kitchen. She could overhear Catherine as she doled out assignments, her authoritative tone reaching all the way to the parlor, where Emily sat. "Hal, I want you on the monitor here to begin with. Like you said, the rain might interfere with your recordings, so let's wait to see if the storm dies down. Andy and Annie, you take your own room to start. Blake and I will sit in our room. Here are the toys, so pick one and take it with you."

Emily got up and headed toward the kitchen, ready to ask the group if they wanted her to turn off the air conditioner. It would get uncomfortably warm if she did that, but at the same time, no one would confuse the sound of the fan turning on as something paranormal.

When she reached the open kitchen door, Emily paused on the threshold, not wanting to cram into the room with everyone else. "Care to join us?" Hal asked.

Emily had just opened her mouth to respond when a high, loud screeching sound began.

The sound persisted for a full ten seconds, and everyone clamped their hands over their ears. Emily even shut her eyes tight, as if that could somehow keep the sound out. It felt like her skull was vibrating.

Once the house was silent again, everyone dropped their hands and looked around. "Where did that sound come from?" Andy asked. Annie had stepped closer to him, her head swiveling as she looked for its source.

"I don't know," Emily answered. "It was so loud that it just seemed to come from everywhere at once."

"But you said the most active ghosts aren't here," Catherine pointed out. "Surely the ghost of the child didn't do that."

Emily shook her head. "They aren't here. And that's the third time I've heard that noise since they left, but a friend of mine had convinced me it probably wasn't paranormal." And, Emily told herself, the sound hadn't been so loud those first couple of times. The quieter screeching noises definitely could have been explained away as something fairly ordinary. But, this time, the way the sound radiated through the house and lasted for so long, she knew it wasn't just a branch squeaking against a window or something similarly mundane.

Blake's eyes lit up, and he pumped a fist. "Yes! A new

haunting to investigate! We might be the first ghost hunters to make contact with something new at this place."

Soon, all five of Emily's guests started chattering at once. Emily waited for a pause in the excited babble to wish them luck with all her heart. Clearly, she did have a new resident, and she was anxious to know a little more about whom they were and whether or not they were friendly.

After that initial excitement, the next few hours were actually dull. Emily did a little cleaning in the dining room, sat in the parlor with a book, and finally went into the kitchen to make herself some dinner. Hal's shift monitoring the video feeds at the kitchen table had ended after an hour. Now, it was Annie who was seated there, a bored look on her face.

"Nothing yet, I guess?" Emily asked as she pulled a loaf of bread toward her so she could make a sandwich. She would have preferred to eat a proper dinner, but she was worried the noise of cooking might be mistaken for ghostly banging on the team's tape recorders.

"Not a thing." Annie paused a moment, then said, "Why would you have a new ghost here? Did someone else die?"

"Not that I know of."

"Did something follow you home?"

Annie had said it casually, but Emily felt the skin on her arms break out in goosebumps. Remembering Annie's reaction to the screeching noise earlier, Emily simply said, "I suppose it's possible." She kept her tone light, determined not to let her own suspicions show.

Shortly before nine o'clock, Catherine called over the radios that had been distributed to the members, telling everyone to meet up in the kitchen. Emily had already eaten and had finally settled in at the kitchen table next to Blake, who had taken over from Annie. He had returned to his usual quiet demeanor, but he was friendly enough as they chatted about their various encounters with ghosts.

Catherine had only called a halt to the investigation to ask what kind of pizza everyone wanted for dinner. Once she had called in an order, the group began comparing notes as they waited for the delivery.

"I'm not having any luck so far," Andy said. "Our room feels totally normal. It's your room, Cath, that gives me the heebie-jeebies. I feel like someone is watching me when I'm in there."

Emily felt a stab of disappointment. She had thought the room felt so much better, but apparently some negative energy was still lingering in the room that had once been Jaxon's. She sighed softly. *Jaxon's room.* No matter how hard Emily tried to think of it as room one, as she used to, she just couldn't separate it from its former guest.

Hal stood. "I'm going upstairs to begin listening to some of my recordings. I'll start with the ones from that room. Holler when the pizza arrives."

The other guests went to the parlor, while Emily stayed in the kitchen. She didn't think they would mind her being there, but at the same time, she liked to give her guests privacy. She was in the middle of preparing coffee for the next morning when she heard a door slam upstairs and a shout from Hal. "Guys! Get up here!"

Emily heard four pairs of feet running up the stairs, and then she heard quieter steps coming back down. "Emily?" Hal called. "I think you should come, too."

Hal was waiting halfway down the stairs, his fingers drumming the banister rapidly. As soon as Emily reached him, he turned and climbed the stairs two at a time. Emily hurried after him.

By the time Emily reached Hal's room, he was already sitting on the bed. A laptop with a pair of headphones plugged into it was next to him. The others were gathered in a tight circle around the bed.

Hal unplugged the headphones. "I want everyone to hear this EVP." He pressed a key on his laptop, and soon his own voice could be heard loudly, asking, "If you're here, will you please come say something?"

There was a long pause, punctuated by a sound that might have been distant thunder, and then a voice began to speak. The words were muffled, and they had an odd rhythm, but the urgency in them was clear. After about five seconds, the silence returned, and Hal stopped the recording.

Thoughts began to rush through Emily's mind. *There's a ghost in my house, and they sound like they need help. Is it Scott? Is it someone else? How did they get here? What do they need from us?*

Emily realized someone was calling her name, and she blinked, trying to refocus her mind on the people right in front of her. "What?"

"I asked if you know who this could be," Catherine said.

"Could it be your husband?" Hal asked gently.

Emily spread her hands. "I have absolutely no idea who this could be or why they're here. I can't even tell if it's a male or a female voice, and it sounds so odd. Could any of you make out actual words?"

Everyone shook their heads as Hal plugged the headphones in again. "Let's all have a listen with these, and maybe we can discern some of the words."

One by one, each guest took a turn listening to the recording with the headphones. No one could make out the words. When it was Blake's turn, he asked Hal to replay the clip three times. Finally, he pulled the headphones off, frowning. "The words are more than just muffled. It's like they're distorted somehow."

It was Emily's turn next, and she sat on the edge of the

bed and slid the headphones on. The voice sounded eerie in this way, like it was inside her head rather than a mere recording. The voice sounded even more urgent as it boomed loudly in her ears, but she couldn't make out a single word. The cadence was off, and there was even something in the tone that sounded mildly threatening. Was the ghost angry at them?

Everyone was still discussing the mysterious EVP when the pizza arrived. Annie asked Emily to join them, but she declined, saying her sandwich had been enough. In truth, she was ready to be alone for a while so she could try to sort through all her questions about this new ghost. Once she said good night and retreated to her bedroom, the question that rose above all the others was whether or not this entity was dangerous.

Emily stood still and closed her eyes, focusing on taking slow, even breaths. She didn't feel nervous. She also hadn't felt watched in Jaxon's room, and she wondered what had caused Andy to feel that way in there. It was the same room where Hal had gotten the recording, so had the ghost only been in there for a short period of time?

Jaxon's ghost had crossed over, so the feeling couldn't be coming from him. Besides, they had saged the whole house, including that room, to clear out any lingering negative energy. And then, since the room had still felt off to Emily, she had added several of the antiques she had bought. The gilt mirror looked so pretty in the corner, and it brightened up the room so nicely. Emily sighed in disappointment. *And here I thought the mirror made the room feel better.*

Emily's eyes snapped open as she gasped. "Something is haunting the mirror!"

8

Emily threw open her bedroom door and ran into the kitchen, where Catherine and Blake were both sitting at the table while the others investigated upstairs. "The mirror!" Emily nearly shouted. When they both just stared at her, she took a breath and continued in her normal voice, "I think the mirror is haunted. The one upstairs in your room. I just bought it on Sunday, and that's when the screeching noises started. I also thought I heard some shouting a few times, but it was really distant, and I passed it off as just my imagination. I should have listened to my gut. I've been hearing the ghost for three days now, and I was in total denial about it."

Blake immediately lifted his radio to his lips. "Everyone come down to the kitchen, right now." His voice was firm, but his smile was broad.

Once everyone was gathered in the kitchen, Emily repeated her theory that the mirror was haunted. She knew ghosts could attach themselves to objects—after all, Kelly had gotten into Eternal Rest because she was attached to her necklace, which Reed had found and given to Emily. Of all the antiques Emily had bought on Sunday, it made the most sense that the mirror was haunted. Yes, she told herself, it was possible the lamp or one of the smaller items was haunted, but the mirror seemed much more likely.

Guests who came to Eternal Rest to investigate paranormal activity were always excited about trying to establish contact with the ghosts there, but being the first group to talk to a brand-new ghost—new to Eternal Rest, at least—added even more enthusiasm. Emily's guests gave up trying to investigate the other rooms and decided to concentrate on Jaxon's room.

As Catherine began assigning roles once again, Emily wished the group good luck and returned to her bedroom. She was so wound up she didn't even feel like sleeping, and she lay in bed for a full hour, wondering at the strange luck of buying a haunted mirror.

Emily normally served breakfast at seven o'clock, but the night before, she had asked her guests what time they preferred, and they had requested ten o'clock. That meant the first round of coffee was for Emily alone, since she was up at her usual hour. The house was silent as she sat down at her desk with a cup of coffee. She had woken up many times to the sounds of her guests talking quietly or moving between Jaxon's room and the kitchen, but they seemed to have turned in around two o'clock in the morning.

Usually, Emily would enjoy that quiet time before everyone woke up. She could check reservation requests, read emails, and just enjoy a little time to herself before the house came alive. On this occasion, though, she was too anxious to know what had happened after she had gone to bed. She hadn't woken up to any shouting, but she hoped her ghost had produced something for her guests.

It was well after ten by the time Andy and Annie came downstairs, still yawning. They reported the night had been quiet, though Hal had optimistically kept his tape recorder on for a full three hours. Between that and the video camera set up in the room, they hoped to hear something more from the ghost when they reviewed it all.

Disappointed, Emily returned to her desk after putting a fresh carafe of coffee in the dining room. She had already put trays of meats, cheeses, and Grainy Day Bakery bagels and muffins on the sideboard. Emily figured her guests wouldn't notice one of the bagels had gone missing. Having a new ghost had worked up her appetite.

By eleven, everyone had finally made it downstairs for breakfast. Instead of heading out to explore Oak Hill like most guests would, this group stayed put, anxious to begin reviewing the hours of video footage and tape recordings from the investigation. They settled into the dining room, each armed with a laptop, headphones, and digital clips to review.

Emily used the time to go upstairs and clean the rooms. She saved Jaxon's room for last. As she walked in, she said softly, "Hello, new guest. Welcome to Eternal Rest Bed and Breakfast. We heard you talking last night, and we hope we'll be able to help you." She continued talking to the ghost while she made the bed, trying to sound conversational as she described the other ghostly residents and promised she would get Sage out there soon to try to establish a connection. Emily hadn't called her yet to fill her in, because she was hoping to have more details after her guests finished their work downstairs.

Before she left the room, Emily walked to the mirror and stood in front of it. "Are you in there?" she asked. The sunlight glinted off the glass, and she squinted.

Something moved behind her.

Emily whirled around, but the room was empty. Her heart racing, she turned back to the mirror, but the only thing moving in it was her own reflection. Emily bent forward at the waist until her face was just inches away from the surface of the mirror.

This time, she could tell the movement came from something human-shaped, though it was nearly transparent. It was like a glimmer of light, something shimmering softly in front of the dresser that stood against the wall behind her. Again, Emily turned to see what was there, but she could see no movement.

She focused on the mirror again. "Are you in the room, or are you still in there?"

Of course, there was no answer. Emily turned and headed downstairs. She reached the hallway before she realized how unusually silent the house was. Conscious of how much noise she was making herself, she tiptoed to the dining room and peered in. All five of her guests stood in a tight circle, their heads bent forward. After a few seconds, Emily heard a muffled voice, then Catherine's sharp intake of breath.

Annie's head lifted as she heard Emily's quiet step. "Come listen," she said breathlessly.

The group made room for Emily to join them around Hal's laptop, and he grinned at her. "There are three separate EVPs here. I've put them all into one audio file."

Emily listened as the recording played. Three times she heard the same unsettling voice from the night before. It still sounded urgent and odd, and again, she couldn't make out any of the words. She shook her head after the last clip ended. "He's talking in such a strange way," she said. "It almost reminds me of a record playing backward."

"Maybe…" Blake began.

Five pairs of eyebrows raised in his direction, and he cleared his throat awkwardly. "Maybe he is speaking backward. He's in a mirror, right? That means his world is flipped, a reflection of ours. So, maybe his words are coming out flipped, too."

Emily had to admit the idea had merit. Hal was already typing away on his laptop, and after a few moments, he said, "I reversed the audio. Let's see how it sounds now."

This time, the voice sounded more natural, the cadence clearly that of someone speaking English. Blake's hunch had been right.

Catherine sighed. "We still can't understand him, though."

"But we're making progress," Blake said. He looked like he was standing a little taller, proud of his break-through with the mysterious voice.

"We're making progress in another way, too," Emily said. "When I was up there cleaning, I saw something in the mirror." Haltingly, she described what she had seen, unable to really put it into words. By the time she finished, her guests were all smiling. They thanked her, then trooped upstairs with plans to camp out in front of the mirror for the remainder of the afternoon. The fact it was daytime, they declared, clearly made no difference. Catherine even speculated the sunshine was helping make the ghost visible.

With that, Emily suddenly found herself alone again. She was invited to join the spectral stakeout, but she figured the room would be crowded enough with five people. Instead, Emily retreated into her bedroom and called Sage. The call went to voicemail, which wasn't surprising since it was the middle of the day, and Emily knew Sage was probably busy with clients at Seeing Beyond. Emily left a message, saying only that there was definitely a new ghost at Eternal Rest, and that it was not, in fact, the entity from the lake.

It wasn't until she said it out loud that the reality of that fact really sank in, and Emily felt a wave of relief wash over her. So far, it appeared this was just a regular old haunting.

Emily felt oddly useless during the afternoon. She didn't want to run errands in town, leaving a house full of guests, but at the same time, there was only so much she could do around the house that would be quiet enough not to interfere with the investigation happening upstairs. Finally, at a loss for anything else to do, she went for a walk in Hilltop Cemetery. When she went there for fresh air and a little exercise, she always walked through the gate and stayed on the main path all the way to the top of the hill. From there, she would walk the uppermost path that circled the hill, then work her way down to the next ring path, and the next, eventually making six loops of the entire hill.

There was no sign of Reed today, and Emily guessed he was working at Oak Hill Memorial Garden, the modern cemetery across town. Emily much preferred the Victorian splendor of what she thought of as "her" cemetery, with the ornate statues, big mausoleums, and so many plants and trees that it felt more like a park than a resting place for the dead. It was hot again, but the oak trees provided plenty of shade as Emily moved along the paths. The magnolia trees were blooming, their huge white flowers sending out a strong, sweet perfume.

Halfway down, Emily stopped and sat down on a bench that looked over the northern horizon. She felt her shoulders relax as the fragrant air and warm sun combined to lull her into a drowsy daze.

I've been so busy lately. If I could just have a break, even a few days to myself...

As Emily's eyes fluttered closed, she heard a sound that had a metallic ring to it. She realized it sounded like an angry fist pounding on the iron door of a mausoleum. Now wide awake, Emily leaned forward and listened for the sound, but the cemetery was silent again.

Fear flooded through Emily. Was it too silent? She

listened for a few seconds that felt like minutes, until a mockingbird began its chatter. Sitting back, relieved, she continued to listen. She had already passed most of the mausoleums, which were arrayed across the upper portion of the hill. She got up and retraced her steps until she was at the top once again, but Emily didn't see anyone.

It was probably the wind, Emily told herself firmly. *Maybe an animal.* And even if it was a ghost, she decided, so what? That was no big deal, and she already knew Hilltop had at least a few spectral residents.

Determined not to let the strange incident spook her, Emily restarted her walk, beginning again with the topmost ring path. She was just leaving the cemetery when she saw Trish's car pulling into the driveway, there to deliver the baked goods for the next morning's breakfast. Emily hurried and called to Trish before she could ring the doorbell.

"Emily, hey! Whew, you startled me!" Trish said, spinning around as Emily came up the front porch steps. "It's been a weird day."

"How so?"

"That's the weirdest part! Do you ever have those times when things just feel, you know, off? Like something's not right, and you can sense it, even though you can't see it."

Emily was nodding as she replied, "Oh, yeah. I've gotten that feeling with ghosts, but my mom calls that the Stovetop Spookies. She says it's the feeling you get when you accidentally left the stove on, and your subconscious knows it."

"Except I didn't leave my stove on. I'm hoping a relaxing night will make the feeling go away. I already sent Clint to pick up dinner for the family. No cooking for me tonight!"

Emily and Trish continued to talk, turning to some local gossip, when someone began to scream.

9

Without stopping to think about what she was doing, Emily shoved her way past Trish and shot into the house. She ran up the stairs and headed straight for Jaxon's room, knowing that was where the scream must have come from. It wasn't until Emily was banging on the door that she heard a loud exhale behind her.

"What's going on?" Trish sounded scared and excited, even though she was breathing heavily from the run up the stairs.

"We've got a new ghost here. I don't know what it did to make someone scream."

Hal opened the door just as Trish's cell phone rang. Even as she asked Hal what was wrong, Emily was aware that Trish was swearing softly behind her.

"It's okay. We're okay," Hal said. He had a tape recorder in his hand, and he was turning it over and over nervously.

"Who screamed? And why?" Emily asked as she sidled past Hal so she could get into the room. Annie was sitting on the bed, looking dazed, while Andy rubbed her back, his head bent toward hers.

Emily felt a hand grab her forearm, keeping her from moving farther into the room. She was surprised to see it was Trish holding her back. "You know I said I've had a weird feeling all day? Well, that call was from the security company. My alarm at the bakery is going off."

"Oh, no. Do you think someone broke in?" Emily immediately ceased thinking about her own troubles as she worried about Trish's.

"It was just a motion detector inside that tripped the alarm, not the door or window sensors. Still, just in case, I'm having the police go check it out. I'm going to meet them over there. I feel like I need to be there to make sure the stove is turned off, you know?"

"Of course. We'll catch up later. I hope it's nothing, Trish."

"Me, too." With that, Trish spun on her heel and hurried toward the stairs. Emily hoped the motion detector simply had a bad sensor. Maybe a spider had crawled in front of it and set it off.

At the moment, though, Emily had her own strange situation to deal with. Turning back to Hal, she simply looked at him expectantly. He nodded, as if he guessed she already knew what he would say. "We saw it, Emily. The ghost."

"Is Annie okay?" Now Emily was eyeing the young woman, who looked pale and shaken but unharmed.

"Yeah, she was just startled. Nothing has happened all afternoon, and we were about to give up, when suddenly the ghost just popped up in the mirror. It was like you described it, sort of a human-shaped glow."

"What was it doing?"

It was Catherine who answered. She had been kneeling next to Annie, but she stood and walked over to Emily. "It looked like the ghost had been pushed." Catherine brought her hands up to form a little rectangle with her fingers. "You know how in a movie, or on TV, someone pushes someone else, but it happens off-camera? The person who was pushed comes flying onto the screen, sort of leading

57

with their shoulders and back, their arms flailing. Even though we can't really see details of this ghost, that's what it seemed like to me."

"Staggering," Blake said quietly. "They just staggered into view, like they were drunk or, like Catherine said, falling over."

"What happened next?" Emily asked.

Catherine rolled her eyes impatiently. "That was it. The ghost disappeared after Annie screamed."

"I'm sure it was frightening to see it so suddenly like that," Emily said, feeling the need to defend Annie's outburst. If she had been up there with them, she might have screamed, too.

"We're going to keep watching," Annie said, her voice shaky but a determined look on her face.

"Let's split up," Catherine suggested. "Andy and Annie, you two take a break. Hal, why don't you start going over your recordings to see if we got any more EVPs? Blake and I will watch the mirror for the next hour, then we can all switch."

The rest of the group agreed immediately, and Emily wondered if they had chosen Catherine as their leader, or if she had simply decided the job should be hers.

"Keep me posted," Emily said. "I'll make a fresh pot of coffee. I've got some baked goods for tomorrow morning, but maybe we should dive into them now."

That suggestion raised a smile from Annie, and Andy was quick to say she needed to eat something after her scare. He held her hand all the way down the stairs and into the kitchen.

Once she served some bagels and biscuits, Emily texted Trish to ask what was happening at Grainy Day. About twenty minutes passed before Trish finally responded, and Emily felt herself relax when she saw the message that everything was fine. The front and back doors of the bakery had still been locked, so clearly, no one had actually been inside.

Just a glitch, Trish had texted.

Emily had to wonder if Trish was also developing some kind of psychic skills, but instead of being able to communicate with the dead, hers was the gift of premonition. Had Trish's strange feeling all day been some kind of foresight about the false alarm?

Or, Emily wondered, did Trish have a new ghostly resident, too? Eternal Rest and the boathouse at Lake Otto both had new ghosts, so maybe Grainy Day did, too. Emily made a mental note to tell Sage about the bakery's odd activity.

Thinking of Sage reminded Emily that her friend hadn't called back yet, which was surprising. She tried calling again and was disappointed when she heard Sage's voicemail message on the other end. Emily was just hanging up when Hal came downstairs. He had his radio in his hand, and he waved it at Emily. "Hey, Catherine says they saw something again!"

"That's great! Hopefully she and Blake will be able to make some sense of what's going on."

Hal began to go back up the stairs, but his radio crackled, and Catherine's voice came out of it, saying, "We need all hands on deck in here. Bring Emily, too."

Emily didn't have to be told twice. She dashed up the stairs behind Hal as Andy and Annie hurried out of the kitchen to join them.

Blake was already standing at the door to the room, one finger pressed against his lips. Emily wasn't sure if they were hearing noise from the ghost and wanted silence, or if they were afraid loud noises might scare it off, like Annie's scream seemed to have done.

Catherine seated on the floor in front of the mirror, her legs crossed and her chin propped on her hands. She was staring at the mirror, rapt. The only light in the room was coming from the bathroom. The door had been pulled almost closed, so only a dim light escaped.

Blake leaned toward Emily and whispered, "When it's dark like this, it's easier to see the glow of the ghost. Guess we should have waited for nightfall, after all."

Emily and Hal sat down on the bed behind Catherine while Blake sat on the floor next to her. Andy and Annie remained standing, stopping just inside the door to keep some distance between themselves and the mirror.

There was nothing in the mirror at the moment, except the dim reflection of everyone and everything in the room. Blake reached forward and grasped the bottom edge of the mirror frame. He shook it gently. As the mirror's movement stopped, a soft glow emanated from the far left side of the glass. Just as Catherine had described before, a glimmering form in the shape of a human came into view, but the movements were jerky. The form staggered, fell, then got up. It stood for a moment, swaying slightly, then rocked backward before staggering again.

The ghost just got hit in the face, Emily thought.

The ghost swayed again, then took several stuttering steps backward before falling to the ground, the top half of its body outside the frame of the mirror.

A second later, the prone body disappeared from the floor. Thinking the ghost was done with its performance, Emily began to relax when the glow suddenly materialized again, taking up almost the entire width of the mirror. In the darkness, the vague form of a face could be seen, the mouth open and yelling. Emily jumped in surprise, and she understood why Annie had been startled enough to scream earlier. Distantly, Emily thought she could actually hear shouting, but it sounded like it was coming from somewhere deep or underwater.

After a few seconds of shouting, the mirror went dark, its glass once again showing only six shocked faces.

There was silence for a long time as everyone waited to see if something more would happen. When the ghost didn't appear again, Catherine said slowly and dramatically, "I think we're seeing the ghost's death. I think it's reliving its final moments, trapped here in this mirror."

Emily closed her eyes briefly. She wanted her instinct to be wrong, but somehow, she knew she should trust what she was feeling. "No," she said in a matter-of-fact tone. "We're not seeing its death. We're seeing its murder."

Emily felt a sinking sensation as she said the words. She knew it was the truth, and she knew she felt obligated to help yet another ghost.

At least, she reminded herself, *it's still better than that boathouse entity.*

The ghost hunters were staring at Emily, mouths open. Annie had pressed her fists against her face, only her wide eyes visible above them. Catherine looked excited, while Blake and Hal both looked slightly disconcerted. Andy was the only one not looking at Emily. His concerned attention was focused on Annie.

"Do you really think this is the ghost of someone who was murdered?" Catherine stood and began pacing back and forth. "This is amazing! We can be the first paranormal investigation team to help solve one of the murders at Eternal Rest!"

"Whoa!" Emily said, raising her hands. "First of all, there haven't actually been any murders in this house. Second, while I would love your help, it might not be easy to track down answers. We can't even understand anything this ghost is trying to tell us."

Catherine stopped pacing and faced Emily, her chin held high. "I have confidence in us!"

Before Emily could respond, her phone rang. She

looked down and was relieved to see it was Sage. "Y'all, I need to take this. Sage is a psychic medium, and if you want to get answers, she's a good place to start."

Emily walked out of the room as she brought the phone to her ear. "Sage?"

"It's been a weird day, Em."

"Trish said the exact same thing to me. I assume your weird day was also because of unusual paranormal activity?"

"Yeah. Something was raising a ruckus in the hallway outside my office. That's never happened before. What happened to Trish?"

"I'll fill you in on that later, but first, I think—no, I know—we have another murder on our hands."

"Are you referring to your new resident? Tell me everything!"

It didn't take much work for Emily to convince Sage to simply come over to hear the details, but Sage insisted on waiting until the next morning. "I have a bit of open time between clients tomorrow," Sage said. "I'm not going to lie: I feel worn out today. Not physically but mentally and spiritually. It's like something has been sucking my energy. I need dinner and bed before I'm ready to try communicating with another ghost."

Emily was fine with that plan; her own stomach was telling her it was time for dinner. She relayed the plan to her guests after wishing Sage a restful night, and they seemed eager for the break, too. Emily offered to cook dinner for everyone, but they declined, saying they wanted to visit a restaurant in Oak Hill. Before long, Emily was alone in the house, cooking dinner for herself. She decided a quiet evening was exactly what she needed. She ate, took a hot bath, and was in bed with a book by the time she heard her guests return.

Emily woke up on Thursday morning with a distinct sense of purpose. She had felt dread when she realized the ghost had been killed, and they were witnessing its final moments, but after a good night's sleep, she felt ready to help yet another spirit find peace.

Sage wasn't due to arrive at Eternal Rest until ten thirty that morning, so as soon as she had gotten breakfast ready, Emily looked up the phone number for the antique store where she had bought the mirror. Finding out where it had come from would be a big step toward finding out who was haunting it.

It was still early, and Emily wasn't surprised when the shop's answering machine picked up. She left a vague message, not wanting to admit her true purpose just yet, then returned to the kitchen for another cup of coffee.

At five minutes after eight, the phone rang, and Emily was delighted when she answered to hear the voice of Sharon Mackie, the owner of Everything Old is New Again. "Emily, good morning! I hope everything is okay with those pieces you bought?"

"Hey, Sharon. Yes, everything is great. I was actually hoping you could tell me where the mirror came from."

Emily could hear the surprise in Sharon's voice as she answered, "Oh, let me look it up. Hang on a minute. You're sure everything is okay with it?"

"Actually, I think it's haunted." Emily's cheeks warmed, and she realized she was blushing. She was used to being a bit of an oddity in Oak Hill for her belief in ghosts, but sometimes it still felt awkward.

Thankfully, Sharon was a believer, too. "That's no surprise. You'd be amazed at the activity we get here. The stories I could tell you about antique beds… Oh! Here we go. That mirror came from Stella Greene. You know the

Greenes over on the east side of town? Stella sold off a lot of things when she decided to go live with her son, Beau. You want the number?"

"That would be wonderful, thank you!"

The second Emily said goodbye to Sharon, she called the number for Stella. It was a man who answered, and when Emily asked to speak to Stella, he explained that his mother's hearing was so bad these days she couldn't really talk on the phone.

"Oh," Emily said, crestfallen. "I had hoped to ask her about an antique mirror she used to own. It's at my house now—at Eternal Rest Bed and Breakfast—and I was hoping to learn more about its history."

"Why don't you come over? She loves visitors, and it's a lot easier to shout at her in person than on the phone!" Beau rattled off his address as Emily jotted it down on the paper she always left out for Kelly. It was early enough that Emily figured she could get over there, talk to Stella, and make it back before Sage arrived.

Emily's guests still hadn't come downstairs, so Emily wrote a note for them, explaining where she was going, and left it sitting in the middle of the dining room table. She figured they would find it there when they came down for breakfast.

The Greene home was on the opposite side of Oak Hill from Eternal Rest, and the town's little bit of rush-hour traffic slowed Emily down. She anxiously tapped her fingertips against the steering wheel as she crawled around the downtown square.

Finally, Emily was on the other side of downtown, heading in the opposite direction as everyone else. The Greenes lived in a large new house in a sprawling subdivision about five miles outside Oak Hill, and Emily had no problem finding it.

It was Beau who answered the door and ushered Emily

inside with a pleasant smile. He looked like he was in his late fifties, and the silver streaks in his dark hair gave him a dashing look. "Your timing today is good," he said. "My client this morning canceled at the last minute, which is why I'm still home. Come on in. Mom is in the living room."

Beau led the way to a large living room, where a tiny old woman sat sipping tea on the couch. She had the TV volume turned up so loud Emily expected every word of the morning news could be heard in the attic. Beau picked up a remote control and muted the TV. "Mom!" He spoke loudly but kindly. "This is Emily."

The woman looked up, and Emily could see the confusion in her eyes, which were the same shade of gray as her hair.

"Hi, Mrs. Greene," Emily said, mimicking Beau's volume. "I wanted to talk to you about an antique gilt mirror you used to own."

Stella stared blankly at Emily for a few more seconds, then she brightened. "Oh, right! Beau told me you were coming. Sorry, dear, sorry. The old mind, you know."

Emily sat down on a chair while Beau excused himself and left the room. "Thank you for letting me come visit," Emily began. "I would like to know where that mirror came from, if you remember."

Stella looked at Emily shrewdly. "Why, because it's haunted?"

Emily gasped, and Stella laughed, slapping a frail hand against her leg. "I knew it! You've heard the strange noises, too, then? That horrible scratching? I was actually glad when my hearing started to go."

"If you knew it was haunted, and you hated the sound, then why didn't you get rid of the mirror sooner?"

Stella shrugged dismissively. "Because it was pretty, and

it looked perfect in my bedroom." She was smiling still, and Emily knew there was more she was excited to tell.

"Do you know who's haunting it?"

"I have an idea. I bought that mirror at an estate sale. Specifically, the one at the Bowers mansion."

The name sounded familiar to Emily, and she could tell she was missing something important by the way Stella was looking at her. "Sorry," Emily said. "That name doesn't mean anything to me."

Stella laughed again, and she raised a finger like she was lecturing a class. She spoke slowly, dramatically. "The estate sale was held after the Bowers twins did each other in."

Emily blinked. Whatever she had expected Stella to say, it wasn't that. When she failed to respond, Stella continued. "You must be too young to remember that scandal. It happened, oh, twenty, twenty-five years ago. They were horrible people, the twins. No one was sad when they killed each other. They had been fighting over the inheritance since before their father ever died, and once he was gone, it just got nastier. They killed each other within six months of their father's death. Judy always said she should get the house because she was the oldest by a matter of minutes. Jerry claimed his father wanted the house to pass to the son. They were the hottest gossip in Oak Hill back then."

Emily admitted she had never heard the story, even though she had lived in Oak Hill her entire life. At the most, she would have been a teenager when it happened, and back then, she probably wouldn't have cared about a couple of bitter adult siblings fighting over an inheritance.

Stella sat back, her satisfied smile still in place. "You'll find plenty of old newspaper articles about it. Let me tell you, sometimes I can't even remember what day it is, but that story is burned into my brain. I've told Beau he's lucky to be an only child because there's no one to fight with him over my stuff when I'm dead."

Emily smiled at the idea of the old woman saying that to her son. Judging by the size of Beau's house, he didn't need to worry about how much money he would inherit from his mother. Emily thanked Stella several times before leaving, and she was thoughtful on the drive home. Not only had Emily found out where the mirror had come from, but she had narrowed down who could be haunting it. Obviously, the spirit of one of the Bowers twins had gone into the mirror. Now, Emily, Sage, and the First Coast Ghost Hunters simply had to figure out which one it was.

And, more importantly, Emily told herself, they had to find out why one of the twins was haunting the mirror. She had thought this was another murder to solve, but if the twins had killed each other, and the whole town already knew about it, then this wasn't a ghost trying to get justice. What, then, did the ghost want? What was it saying in that urgent tone on Hal's recordings, and why had it seemed to be yelling at them in the mirror?

If the ghost wasn't asking for help trying to find its killer, then it was clearly in some other kind of trouble.

11

Emily got home just five minutes before Sage was supposed to arrive. Catherine immediately came bounding out of the dining room to ask if she had any news. In that moment, Emily understood Stella's delight in revealing the dramatic tale of the Bowers twins, but she said she was waiting until Sage arrived so she only had to tell the story once.

Emily wasn't surprised when the doorbell rang right at ten thirty, but she was surprised to open it to see not just Sage but Trevor, too. Sage said good morning and whisked through the door, past Emily, and right into the dining room, ready to get to work while Trevor followed sheepishly, one hand running nervously through his dark hair. "Hope you don't mind," he said. "Sage asked if I could take my lunch break early today to come help."

"Actually, I'm glad you're here," Emily said. "This mystery is more, well, mysterious than I originally thought. It will be good to have an extra mind working on it."

Just as Emily turned to follow Trevor into the hallway, she heard a step on the porch. "Wait for me," she heard Reed drawl. She looked over her shoulder to see Reed smiling at her. His gray sweatshirt had streaks of red Georgia clay on it, and he brushed his fingers along it to no avail. "I've been trying to level part of the Jones plot all morning," he explained. "Sage asked me to take my lunch break early today so I could come here, but she won't say why."

"Sage loves to be mysterious," Emily agreed, waving Reed inside.

Emily led Trevor and Reed into the dining room, which was crowded now that there were more people in the party. Everyone gathered around the table after Hal and Andy retrieved the chairs from the kitchen, with Sage sitting at one end and Emily at the other. Sage introduced herself to the ghost hunters before Emily could, adding, "Sorry about butting in on your investigation, but I really want to know what's happening!" Emily noted that Sage didn't sound sorry at all, and she knew her guests were sincere when they said they were happy to have her insight.

Emily quickly filled Reed and Trevor in on the discovery that the mirror was haunted and the activity they had experienced. Sage waited until she was done, then she folded her hands on the table and gazed at Emily, saying, "You have big news for us, I can tell. Let's hear it!"

Emily began to relay everything Stella had told her, and to her surprise, Sage looked shocked when she mentioned the Bowers name. She paused, one eyebrow raised. "Sage? Does that name mean something to you? I thought it sounded familiar, but I don't remember these twins."

Sage pursed her lips at Emily, and her tone was teasing. "You know that name because you've heard both me and Reed talk about it. I'll give you a pass for not paying attention, since you were dealing with a dead guest at the time. Reed used to sneak into the Bowers mansion when he was a teenager, back when it was vacant. And now that it's been restored, the owners are clients of mine. They refuse to sleep in the master bedroom because of the negative energy in there, along with some other weird things they've experienced. I've always assumed that's where the twins killed each other, but I had no idea one of their ghosts was still around!"

"I vaguely remember that story," Reed said. "That's probably why the mansion was abandoned for a number of years: if the house had been left to two siblings who both died before the inheritance had been sorted out, it would have been in a sort of legal limbo in terms of ownership."

"Which twin do you think is in the mirror?" Trevor asked.

Emily shrugged. "The voice is so muffled that it's impossible to tell. We certainly can't make out any words the ghost is saying."

"And the voice is backwards, we think because everything is reversed in the mirror," Catherine said.

"Actually, I think I can help with that first problem," Sage said. "The ghost probably sounds muffled because there's a layer of glass between us and it. It's no different than someone standing outside your window, trying to talk to you. A way to make it sound better is so simple that it will sound silly, but trust me."

Instead of explaining her plan, Sage got up and headed toward the hallway. A chorus of protests followed her, but it was Emily's voice that rose above the others. "Aren't you going to tell us?"

"Meet me upstairs in the room!" Sage said, turning left toward the kitchen instead of moving to the staircase.

Emily allowed her guests and her friends to go up first, lingering at the bottom of the stairs to wait for Sage, who soon returned from the kitchen. She was holding an empty glass in one hand. When Emily gestured questioningly toward it, Sage said in her best spooky voice, "Do not question the tools of the psychic medium!"

Squeezing everyone into Jaxon's room was tough, and

Emily wound up standing in the open doorway. Trevor came over and stood close to her, keeping his voice low as he said, "You once mentioned that Victorians believed a soul could accidentally get trapped in a mirror. Do you think that's what happened here?"

"That's my guess, though I suppose the ghost could have attached itself to the mirror on purpose. The problem is, we don't know what that purpose could be."

"Hush, you two!" Sage admonished. "Speedboat here is going to start his tape recorder."

"Speedboat?" Emily asked, confused.

Sage nodded her head toward Hal. "He looks like he's dressed for a day on the water, not a day of ghost hunting. Oh, you should have been with us at the boathouse on Sunday. Best of both worlds for you!"

Hal looked like he was torn between feeling offended and laughing. When he caught the amusement in Emily's eyes, he opted for a laugh.

"We're going to hold the rim of the glass against the mirror," Sage explained once the room quieted down. "That should help us get a clearer sound."

"Seriously?" Emily asked.

"You never did that as a kid?" Reed sounded surprised. "I put a glass up to the wall between my room and my sister's whenever she was talking to her best friend on the phone. I'd know if she was planning to sneak out, so I could tell on her and get her grounded."

"You're a terrible brother," Andy said, but he was looking pointedly at Hal.

"I did it one time," Hal said, rolling his eyes.

"And you're about to do it again!" Sage shook her head impatiently. "Hold your tape recorder up right next to the glass. Is it on? I'll start the conversation.

"Hello, there, Bowers twin! Can you hear me? We've come to talk to you again. These people have heard you

72

shouting, and they heard you talking on the tape recorder, but so far, no one has been able to understand you. By using this glass, your voice should come through loud and clear. What do you want us to know?"

Sage paused, and the room was absolutely silent as everyone stared at the mirror.

"Was your twin the one who killed you?" Sage asked.

Catherine waited a moment before saying, "I expect we won't hear anything ourselves. Emily, were you ever in the room when you heard the shouting?"

"No, I was always somewhere else." Emily leaned forward to stare at the mirror. "I don't even see the ghost. Maybe they're out of energy, or uncomfortable around so many people."

"Patience," Sage said. "Bowers twin, why are you still here?"

Sage went on and on with the questions, and as the time passed, everyone began shifting uncomfortably. Emily realized the atmosphere of the room had changed. It felt electrically charged, and the tiny hairs on the back of her neck were prickling. She kept glancing behind her to see if someone was standing in the hallway. Emily knew Sage felt it, probably even more than the rest of them, and when the two exchanged glances, Sage just gave a little nod. Something was about to happen. Emily didn't know if it was her growing mediumship abilities telling her that or her past experience with paranormal activity, but she sucked in her breath and held it in anticipation.

The sound of a woman's deep, raspy voice filled the room. It said only three words, unidentifiable since they were backward, yet extremely clear. When the sentence finished, the glass Sage was holding to the mirror shattered.

Sage jumped, dropping the remains of the glass she

was still holding. Hal threw himself backward, clutching the tape recorder to his chest to protect it. Annie screamed.

Emily simply watched the scene unfold before her. It almost seemed to be happening in slow motion. It was the sight of red against Sage's hand that finally spurred her into action. She turned and dashed down the hall to a closet that had spare towels. Grabbing a few, she rushed back to the room and pushed her way between Andy and Annie so she could reach Sage.

"How bad is it?" Emily asked. She had to shout to be heard above the din of everyone discussing what had just happened.

"Oh, it's not so bad," Sage said, but her voice was shaking. "That was a first for me, though." She held out her hand, and Emily saw that her friend was right: there was only one shallow cut. Emily handed a towel to Sage, then looked down at the floor. The shards of glass were arrayed in an arc, as if the glass had exploded from the inside. A quick glance showed that no one else was injured. Hal's hand had been close to the glass, too, but he had been luckier than Sage.

Catherine's voice cut through the noise. "On the plus side, we know which twin it was! That was definitely a female voice!"

Judy Bowers, then. I wonder where the brother's ghost wound up? Emily glanced at the mirror, but there was no movement in it.

"I'm going to flip this right now to see what she said." Hal nearly ran out of the room in his excitement.

It didn't take Hal long. Emily had just enough time to retrieve her broom and dustpan before he had the audio reversed. He returned to the room with his laptop. "We don't even need headphones to understand this! It's so clear!" He started the recording, and the same woman's voice boomed, "He killed me."

74

Catherine asked Hal to play it again. There was no doubt what the ghost of Judy Bowers was saying. Even as Catherine and Blake high-fived each other in celebration, Emily turned to Sage and said, "I'm glad she confirmed your question from earlier, but this still doesn't tell us why she's haunting the mirror. Why is she sticking around instead of simply crossing over?"

"Maybe she's stuck," Sage speculated, putting her fingertips softly against the surface of the mirror.

"Emily, we were just talking about that old superstition. Did the Victorians know how to get a ghost out of a mirror?" Trevor asked.

"Hopefully the same way you get a ghost to stop haunting any other object," Sage answered. "You find out what it wants or help it understand it's dead, then you help it cross over. We can keep asking questions to find out if she's stuck or sticking around for a reason."

"The more we know about the murder, the better," Annie piped up. "I'd be happy to go to the library to look up old newspaper stories about it."

Emily smiled gratefully at Annie. Not only was the young woman doing them all a favor, but Emily could tell by the look on her face that she was eager to take a break from ghost hunting. Of all of them, she was the only one who seemed to be a little scared. Andy said he would go, too, and they waited only long enough to get Catherine's approval of the plan before heading out.

Reed was eyeing Emily, a small smile on his lips.

"What?" Emily asked self-consciously.

"I'm just waiting to hear what trouble you're about to get yourself into."

"I don't get myself into trouble. I just help spirits get answers." When Reed just raised one eyebrow, Emily continued, "Okay, sometimes it gets me into unusual situations, but I still wouldn't call it trouble. And if you really want to know, I thought I'd start by talking to the neighbors who live near the Bowers mansion. Maybe someone will have helpful information for us."

In truth, Emily knew she was just making up an excuse to get out of the house. She was ready for a change of scenery and a little time to herself. A drive out to the area of the Bowers mansion would be perfect for that.

Reed looked at Emily earnestly. "Be careful," he warned.

"Of what? I'm just going to talk to the neighbors."

"I don't know," Reed answered. "Call it a feeling. And yes, I know, you'll tell me I'm psychic for saying so, but I'm not. I can't explain it, Emily. Just take care."

12

Emily had wanted a nice, relaxing drive across Oak Hill. Instead, she found herself ruminating over Reed's warning. While she had been too busy to work on her own budding skills with any real intensity, Emily had been getting the feeling for a while that Reed either had growing spiritual skills of his own, or he had always had them, and he was finally letting his guard down enough to put them on display from time to time.

The Bowers mansion was in a neighborhood southeast of downtown. It would have been easy to walk from the old house to the grassy square that sat in the middle of Oak Hill. Emily didn't know how old the mansion was, but judging by its wide porch and tall columns, it was even older than Eternal Rest. Emily had never snuck into the place like Reed and his friends did during their teenage years, but she remembered the house and how rundown it had looked. The new owners had clearly put a lot of love —and probably a lot of money, too—into its restoration, and its white paint with springtime-green trim looked warm and inviting. No one would look at the house and suspect a double murder had happened there.

Emily parked her car on the curb between the Bowers mansion and the house to its right. All of the houses in the neighborhood were equally grand, though the architecture varied. The house to the right of the Bowers mansion was Victorian in style, but much fancier than her own home. Eternal Rest was a simple country home, while this house was an ornate (and, as far as Emily was concerned, over-adorned) mansion, complete with a turret at one corner.

Emily rang the bell, but after waiting awhile, she decided no one must be home. She returned to the street and headed for the house on the other side of the Bowers mansion. The property on that side was vast, and the Colonial-style house looked comparatively small on the wide expanse of lawn, even though it was just as big as the neighboring houses. A double staircase arced up to the front door, which was high above the ground.

As Emily walked up the long driveway, she saw the entire back half of the property was surrounded by a tall chain-link fence. The fence looked out of place in the historic neighborhood, but it was easy to see why it had been installed: two potbellied pigs were eyeing Emily lazily as she approached. She could see a few more a short distance away.

Emily chose the staircase to the right and made the climb up to the wide front door. She rang, expecting no one to answer at this house, either. After all, it was the middle of a Thursday, and most people would be at work. She was surprised, then, when a man who looked to be in his late sixties, with gray hair and a deeply-lined, tanned face, answered the door. He was wearing a pair of big black rubber boots, but otherwise he looked like the average retired man.

"Hi," Emily said quickly, caught slightly off-guard. She suddenly realized she had never made a plan beyond "talking to the neighbors," and she didn't actually know where to begin. "Tell me about your neighbors who killed each other" seemed like a bad way to start off. Thinking hard, the best Emily could come up with was, "I'm hoping you might be able to help me. I just bought an antique mirror that used to be in the house next door. I'm hoping to learn a little about the history there."

The man's faded blue eyes squinted doubtfully at Emily. "You live around here?" he asked.

"Yes, I'm Emily Buchanan. I own Eternal Rest Bed and Breakfast."

The man made a quiet "humph," and Emily wasn't sure if he was being judgmental or if he was simply annoyed about having his day interrupted. After peering at her for a long moment, he said, "You can't tell me you don't know what happened in that house."

"The Bowers twins? I just found out about them this morning. I know nothing else about the house."

The man's face relaxed, and he laughed. "And you call yourself local? Come on in. I'm always happy to gossip, and it's been ages since anyone asked about the Bowers place. I'm Jim, by the way. Jim Nelson." He waved Emily inside, adding, "Just let me take these boots off. The wife will holler if she knows I had them on in the house, but I was just coming in the back door when you rang."

Soon, Emily was seated in a living room that looked more rustic than historic. While the house's exterior was grand, the inside reminded Emily more of a barn than a house. There were old, rusted farm tools displayed on the walls, patchwork quilts were draped across the sofa and chairs, and much of the decor had a chicken theme.

Emily was trying not to gawk too much, but Jim seemed to notice, anyway. He sounded amused and slightly apologetic as he said, "Sarah is really into the farmhouse chic look. She's the one who wanted the pigs, too. I guess we should have retired to the country instead of staying here in town. You want a glass of pig milk?"

"What?" Emily's head snapped toward Jim, and she relaxed when she saw his playful smile.

"How about a soda, then?"

"No, but thank you."

"You're an easy guest! Sit down, and tell me what you want to know first." Jim settled onto a recliner, and Emily sat on the sofa, careful to avoid the threadbare—but probably valuable—old quilt.

Emily had taken the few moments as she walked into the house to gather her thoughts, so she felt better prepared to answer Jim's inquiry this time. While she wasn't going to be blunt about the haunted mirror, she wasn't going to lie, either. "My current guests want to know more about the history of a beautiful antique mirror I bought recently. I found out it came from the Bowers estate sale, presumably shortly after the twins' deaths. I realize you probably don't know anything about the mirror itself, but I thought maybe you could tell me something about the family."

"They were a mess," Jim said, the scorn clear in his voice. "Judy and Jerry were quite a bit older than me. When Sarah and I moved in here, old Mr. Bowers was still alive, but the twins had moved in with him. Ostensibly, they had done so to take care of him in his old age. Of course, it quickly became clear they simply didn't want to wait for him to die before they could take over the house. The problem was that both of them wanted sole ownership. They were always fighting. We'd be out back in the field, and you'd hear crashing noises from them throwing things at each other. Sometimes we'd take our dogs out for a walk around the neighborhood, and you'd see them on the front porch, just shouting at each other."

"It's no surprise they killed each other," a voice said from the doorway behind Emily. She craned her head around and saw a tall woman with short gray hair. She looked like she was about the same age as Jim, and Emily was surprised how muscular she looked. Emily surmised that caring for pigs must be a great way to stay in shape. "Hi, I'm Sarah."

Emily could hear the question mark in the introduction, and she quickly explained to Sarah who she was and why she was there. Sarah flopped down on the couch next to Emily and gestured to Jim. "It's true. Those two were awful. Not just to each other but to everyone in their orbit."

"No one in the neighborhood liked them," Jim added.

"Why would they?" There was venom in Sarah's voice. "Judy wanted to parcel off the land and build condos so she could make as much money as she could. Jerry was so selfish that he wanted the house all to himself. He was planning to send Judy packing as soon as Mr. Bowers died."

Jim laughed sardonically. "Well, he did, in a fashion. The trouble is, she sent him packing, too!"

Jim and Sarah both laughed, and Emily managed a small smile. She didn't think murder was funny, but then, she hadn't been forced to put up with the twins as neighbors.

"Why were they so hateful to each other?" Emily asked, wanting to shift the subject away from death humor.

Jim waved a hand. "They were spoiled rotten as kids, I hear. They were always competing with each other, determined to out-do each other in everything. If Judy got a Corvette, Jerry would whine until he got a Porsche. That sort of thing. I don't think there was much hope for them as adults."

"And then," Sarah said, picking up the narrative, "Mr. Bowers got dementia. That was after they were adults, of course, but as his state worsened, he started saying wild things about his will. He swore he had rewritten it to cut them out, and at one point, he even claimed to have left everything to the guy who managed the house for him."

"It sounds like Mr. Bowers realized he had raised kids who didn't deserve a big inheritance," Emily said.

"Maybe," Jim said slowly. "It could have also been that he was just confused and not really sure of what he was saying. As you can imagine, though, it only escalated the twins' animosity."

Sarah got up and went to a bookcase against one wall. When she returned to the sofa, Emily could see she had a photo album in her hands. Sarah flipped through the pages until she pointed a triumphant finger at a photo and shouted, "A-ha! Here it is!" She turned the album toward Emily. "That's him. Wes Gibson. He worked for Mr. Bowers for years."

Emily looked at the photo Sarah was indicating, and she saw a man who might have been in his sixties sitting at a picnic table with a woman Emily recognized as a much-younger Sarah. The man had dark-blond hair and a thick moustache, and he was wearing a navy-blue suit. Sarah was wearing a yellow sundress, and she was smiling broadly at the camera.

"That's the man who ran things for Mr. Bowers?" Emily asked.

"That's him," Sarah said. "He and his family used to come to our Fourth of July cookout, and I could never convince Wes to dress casually. It would be sweltering hot, and he would be sitting there in his suit, never breaking a sweat."

"What happened to him? I assume he had to find a new job after the deaths." Emily liked the look of the guy: he gave the appearance of being friendly but firm, someone who could get difficult tasks accomplished without ever losing his smile.

Jim snorted in a sort of laugh. "He had to find a new job long before that. Those twins made life a living hell for him the second they moved back in. Of course, I expect they made things hard for him long before that, too. Poor guy. Mr. Bowers was so kind, but his kids turned out the opposite."

Emily was hardly listening anymore. All she knew was that Wes Gibson sounded like someone who might know why one of the Bowers twins would have a reason to stick around as a ghost rather than crossing over. "Is Mr. Gibson still here in Oak Hill?" she asked, trying to keep her tone casual. She reminded herself that even if he were still alive, he would be very old.

"I'm not sure," Jim said. "After the twins fired him, he just sort of disappeared. We tried calling to check on him and to offer our condolences on losing his job, but our calls always went to his answering machine."

"He wasn't even at Mr. Bowers's funeral, which is really sad," Sarah said. "Wes was the best friend that man had in his later years. He made sure Mr. Bowers was happy and that his house always looked nice. And I'm sure he was better company than the twins."

"Well, thank you for your time," Emily said, rising. "You have both been so helpful. My guests will be excited to know a little more about the family that used to own the mirror."

Except, Emily realized, she really hadn't learned all that much about the Bowers family, except that the father had raised two spoiled children. Still, it was a start, and she hoped this gossipy sort of news combined with anything Annie learned at the library would help them begin to understand why Judy was haunting the mirror.

Emily had walked out of Jim and Sarah's home determined to track down Wes Gibson. By the time she reached her car, Emily had already shifted gears from finding the former manager to finding some food. It was well past lunchtime, and she hadn't stopped to eat, let alone to rest. Emily leaned her head back against the head-rest, closed her eyes, and sighed.

There it is again, she thought. *This strange new independent streak. I feel like I have to do everything myself, and I have to do it now. But I don't. Wes Gibson can wait.*

Just as Emily opened her eyes and started her car, Sage called. She skipped past a greeting to ask, "Where are we going to meet for lunch?"

"You won't be surprised to know I was just thinking about getting something to eat."

"That has nothing to do with being psychic and everything to do with being hungry, because I never had lunch. I figured you were in the same boat. Let's meet at The Depot, and we can fill each other in."

Soon, Emily and Sage were seated at a table inside The Depot, which sat on the square downtown. The restaurant was mostly empty at that hour, and before the two women could exchange information, the owner, Jay, walked over to say hello.

"I might need to have some of your ghost hunters out here to look around," Jay said ominously. "We've had a couple of things go missing in the kitchen the past few weeks, only for them to turn up right where they should be a day or two later. Yesterday morning, when I came in, the sink faucet was going full-blast. I do a check of the restaurant every night, and I'm always the last one out the door. I would never leave the faucet running."

Emily smiled. "I've got lots of ghost hunters staying with me the next few months. I'm sure some of them would be happy to investigate here." *Why are ghosts suddenly showing up in new places?* Emily had never heard of any kind of paranormal invasion before, but there certainly seemed to be a lot of new ghost stories popping up around Oak Hill.

Jay returned to the kitchen after some small talk, and Sage immediately leaned across the table toward Emily. "Judy Bowers spoke to us again!" she said. "She got two sentences out, both crystal clear: 'He killed me. It was him.' What do you think of that?"

"I think she seems very determined to let us know that Jerry killed her. Did you tell her we already know that little tidbit?"

"I did, but you know how ghosts can be. Maybe she's so hung up on the fact that her own brother killed her that she can't think about anything else. Her ghost might still be here because she was so shocked he would do such a thing."

"That's an interesting theory, but when you hear what I have to say, you'll think she's shocked he didn't kill her sooner." Emily filled Sage in on her meeting with Jim and Sarah, and Sage could only shake her head in disgust. After she wrapped up her story, Emily ended with, "Now, I just need to find this Wes Gibson to see what he might know."

"Not today," Sage said in what Emily thought of as her "stern mother" voice. "You're tired. Not just physically but spiritually. I can sense it. I order you to go home and take it easy for the rest of the day."

When Emily tried to protest, Sage raised her fork and brandished it like a sword. "I mean it!"

After such a busy start to the day, the rest of Emily's afternoon was surprisingly quiet. Sage had made her promise three times not to track down Wes Gibson until the next morning, after she had gotten some sleep. Emily still needed to clean her guests' rooms, though, since she had been too busy that morning to do it. When she got back to Eternal Rest, she found her guests gathered in the dining room.

"Don't worry about our room," Catherine said, when Emily said hello to the group and mentioned she would be heading upstairs to clean. "You got the glass cleaned up, and that's all that matters."

"I haven't really made a mess, so no need to clean mine," Hal chimed in.

"Same with us," Andy said. He and Annie were sitting slightly apart from everyone, and Annie was staring at a notebook filled with small, neat handwriting.

A few seconds later, as if her brain had finally caught up to the conversation, Annie raised her head. "Yeah, our room is fine."

Emily nodded at Annie's notes. "Is that all from your trip to the library?"

Annie sat up straighter and smiled proudly. "Yes! I found a lot of interesting information. Those Bowers twins were not well-liked, by anyone. Neighbors called the police on them eight different times over the years. They killed each other just a week before Christmas, twenty-four years ago. Jerry shot Judy, and Judy stabbed Jerry with scissors. Once they were dead, there was no one left to inherit the house. It was tied up in a trust for a while before some distant family finally wound up with it. They decided to sell everything off, which is how you got the mirror, Emily."

"Did the newspaper articles mention which neighbors called the police?" Emily asked, thinking of Jim and Sarah.

Annie glanced at her notes. "No. Oh, also, the house was built in 1869 by Carroll Bowers. The house was in the Bowers family for over a century!"

"Great work, Annie! Thank you!" Emily said warmly. While she had never been interested in joining a team of ghost hunters, she always appreciated the hard work they did just because they were interested in the paranormal. They didn't get paid, and oftentimes, like this week, they were actually paying for the opportunity to investigate.

"We're going to try talking to Judy's ghost later tonight," Catherine said. "We're hoping to get some new information out of her."

"Good luck. Sage made it sound like she's pretty hung up on her murder."

"Can't blame her," Blake said softly.

Emily left her guests to their planning for that night's question-and-answer session with Judy Bowers, heading straight for her desk in the parlor. There were fewer voice-mails than she had expected, so calling people back about reservations was completed quickly. It was Emily's inbox that felt overwhelming, and she spent a couple hours returning messages and confirming reservation requests.

"I can't wait until I have a new assistant," Emily mumbled as she went to the kitchen for her third glass of sweet tea.

The phone rang as soon as Emily got back to her desk, and she sighed. It never stopped. Of course, she reminded herself quickly, busy phones and inboxes meant booked rooms, and that was always a good thing.

"Hello, Eternal Rest Bed and Breakfast," Emily said, answering the phone as she slid into her chair.

"Oh, hi. Um… This is Amanda Leyland. We have reservations from Friday until Sunday?" The voice sounded harried.

"Yes, hi." Emily kept her voice pleasant, but she could tell by Amanda's tone that she had some kind of bad news.

"My husband and his brother both got food poisoning. I told them not to eat those leftovers. I'm afraid we have to cancel our stay with you."

"Is your entire party canceling?" Emily asked. The Leyland family had booked all four rooms, and Amanda had mentioned it was a little family reunion when she had called to book several months before.

"Yes. The three of us were nearly half the group, so it doesn't make sense for any of us to go now."

Emily felt both disappointed and relieved. The family would have to pay their deposit since they were canceling at the last minute, but the full amount would have helped Emily save up more to replace the roof. Even as she thought that, Emily turned and glanced at the water stain on the wallpaper in one corner of the parlor. At the same time, though, not having to get the rooms ready for a new round of guests would be a nice break. Plus, she could use the unexpected free weekend to keep searching for answers to why Judy Bowers was haunting her mirror.

"I'm sorry to hear you can't make it," Emily said. "I hope your husband and brother-in-law feel better soon."

Amanda apologized quickly, but Emily could tell her mind was more on her sick family than on her change of plans. Emily hung up the phone and headed straight into the dining room. "So," she began, as the heads of her five guests looked up at her, "the party who had booked

Eternal Rest this weekend just canceled. Do you all want to stay a couple of extra days? If you're willing to help me with this haunting, then I'm happy to let you stay for free."

It really wouldn't cost that much to let them stay, Emily told herself. Besides, she had already ordered Grainy Day baked goods for each day, so someone may as well be there to eat them.

It took less than thirty seconds for the ghost hunters to enthusiastically accept the invitation. As if in response to the new plans, a muffled shout drifted downstairs.

"I think Judy Bowers is happy you're staying," Emily quipped.

14

Friday morning felt almost celebratory. Instead of checking out, the ghost hunters were getting to stay through the weekend, and Emily knew she would have their enthusiastic help with her new haunting. She even joined the group in the dining room, digging into breakfast alongside them.

Soon, though, it was time for the work to begin. Judy Bowers hadn't done any more shouting the night before, so Hal took his headphones and laptop to the parlor so he could listen for any EVPs on his recordings. Catherine and Blake returned to their room to try communicating again, and Andy and Annie headed back to the library to do more research.

Emily neatened the rooms, with the exception of Jaxon's room. Catherine and Blake still insisted it was fine, and Emily expected they were too eager to talk to Judy's ghost to care about having their bed made.

Once she had cleaned up from breakfast and dusted both the parlor and dining room, Emily sat down at her desk and tried searching online for Wes Gibson. She found someone by that name who had died in New York in 1971, but that was all. Next, Emily tried the phone book. There were several Gibsons listed, but none with the name Wes or Wesley.

As she put the phone book away, the back of Emily's neck grew warm, and a little shudder ran up her spine. She felt like someone was staring at her. Quickly, she whipped her head around, but all she saw was an empty parlor. Hal wasn't even there. He walked in a moment later, a power cord for his laptop in his hand.

"What?" he asked, seeing Emily's expression.

Emily absently rubbed the back of her neck. "I'm not sure. Just an odd feeling, like someone was staring at me."

"Maybe Judy has figured out how to crawl out of the mirror?"

"Ew, don't say that!" Emily said, making a horrified face. "Speaking of Judy, have you found any EVPs yet?"

"No. She might have worn herself out with all the shouting yesterday. I'm about done listening, at least." Hal settled back into his spot on the sofa, and Emily swiveled around to her desk again. The strange feeling was gone now, and she felt better having Hal in the room with her.

Since Andy and Annie were already downtown, the rest of the ghost hunters drove there to find lunch. At first, Emily enjoyed having the house to herself for a while. Since she had gotten a lot done during the morning, she happily sprawled on the sofa with a book.

That relaxed feeling only lasted for a short while. As she read, Emily's eyes kept turning to the parlor windows. The curtains had been thrown open to allow the sunshine to pour in, but suddenly, Emily felt exposed. A little shiver ran along her spine again. Even though she was alone in the house, she didn't feel like it. Maybe, Emily told herself, Judy had escaped the mirror, as Hal had suggested. Even when her usual ghosts were at home, though, Emily never felt like she was being watched, like she did now. If it wasn't Judy, she wondered, then who could it be? Her thoughts went immediately to the boathouse entity.

Feeling both scared and slightly silly, Emily threw her book onto the coffee table and rose quickly. She walked straight to the parlor windows and closed the curtains. She couldn't tell where the watchful feeling was coming from, but she still felt better knowing no one could look in and see her there.

Emily tried to read again, but her brain was too busy wondering why she had been getting the feelings of being watched. Finally, knowing that work was the only thing that could really distract her, she grabbed her cleaning bucket from under the kitchen sink and retreated into her room.

By the time her guests returned, Emily had her bedroom and bathroom gleaming. It hadn't been a relaxing way to spend her time alone, but at least it had been productive.

There was a knock at Emily's bedroom door, and when she answered, she was surprised to see Annie looking pale once again, like she had when she had first heard the phantom shouting. "Are you okay?" Emily blurted.

Annie just nodded and gestured down the hall. "Can you join us in the dining room? We'll fill you in."

Emily followed, and she found the other ghost hunters already seated around the table. It was Hal who spoke first, saying, "You know that feeling you got, Emily? It's not just you. And it's not just happening here."

Annie was nodding. "I felt it at the library, too. Andy had gone to ask for some additional newspaper files, so I was by myself at the microfiche machine. I started getting this feeling"—Annie reached up to touch the back of her head—"like someone was staring at me. There were other people in the library, but this was intense. Not like someone just glancing my way, you know?"

"Did you see anyone?" Emily asked.

"When I turned around, it was just people walking along or looking at books. Is that library haunted?"

"I don't know. I felt the same thing here at the house." Emily sat back in her chair, thinking hard. Could Judy's spirit have somehow followed Annie and Andy? Was the boathouse entity going after her guests?

"Anyway," Annie continued, "we didn't find any additional information today to help us figure out what's going on."

"Still, I appreciate you two volunteering to look," Emily said. "What are all of you doing this afternoon?"

"Trying to talk to Judy some more, of course," Catherine said matter-of-factly.

"But," Blake added quickly, "we were going to ask if we can investigate the cemetery tonight. Since Judy isn't really talking to us all that much, we thought we'd try our luck with some of the other ghosts around here."

"Of course!" Emily said. "I'll take y'all over there whenever you like."

Emily declined the invitation to camp out in front of the haunted mirror. Instead, she sat down in the parlor with her book again. This time, she had no problem getting lost in its pages. Her house was full, she didn't feel like something unseen was staring at her, and she finally allowed herself to completely relax.

It was the ring of her cell phone that finally brought Emily's attention back to the real world. On the other end, Sage sounded concerned. "I'm closing my shop early and heading home," she said. "Something strange is going on."

Emily actually laughed.

"And how is that funny?" Sage asked, clearly annoyed with Emily's reaction.

"It's not funny, but it's *funny*," Emily explained. "Something strange is going on here, too. But before I tell you about our experiences, why don't you tell me about yours?"

"There's actually not much to tell," Sage conceded. "This morning started great: some of my favorite clients were here, I had a lot of energy, and Jen brought me the most delicious lunch. Then, about an hour ago, I started getting this odd feeling."

"Let me guess," Emily broke in. "You felt like someone was staring at you, but no one was there?"

"Yes, precisely!" The surprise was evident in Sage's voice. "I thought maybe an impolite ghost was hanging out with me, but I couldn't sense anything. I was feeling so spooked that when my latest client came in, I jumped at the sound of the door."

"I felt it here, around lunchtime. And then, earlier, one of my guests felt it while she was doing research at the library. What's going on, Sage?"

"I have no idea."

"Do you think it's tied to my new haunting? I thought of the boathouse entity, of course, but honestly, I'm trying even harder to *not* think of it."

Sage was silent for a while, and Emily could picture her friend sitting in her office, her eyes closed and her face slack as she reached out psychic feelers. "It could have something to do with the Bowers twins," Sage said eventually, "but I don't think it's that thing at the lake. The feelings I've been getting today are disconcerting, and definitely spooky, but I don't feel like I'm in danger."

"That makes me feel better."

"I'm glad you're comforted. I don't know what's going on, Em, but I don't like it. I feel like something is coming."

The doorbell rang just as Sage finished her pronouncement, and Emily jumped. "Something is coming," she said, her voice shaking with adrenaline. "Luckily, it's probably just Trish with tomorrow morning's baked goods."

"Call me with any news!" Sage commanded before hanging up.

Emily took a couple of deep breaths as she walked to the front door. She felt silly for reacting the way she had. After all, it was only the doorbell. In her experience, no ghost had ever rung the doorbell before doing something spooky.

It wasn't Trish at the door. It was Trevor. His eyes were wide, but it was from excitement rather than fear. "I came here the second I finished work," he said breathlessly.

"What's going on?" Emily asked as she waved him in and led the way to the parlor.

Emily sat down on one of the wingback chairs, but Trevor paced back and forth behind the sofa. "I was telling a guy I work with about your haunting," Trevor said, glancing at Emily almost apologetically. "I figured it wasn't a secret, and since he's a lifelong Oak Hill resident, I thought maybe he would have some interesting stories about the twins. Well, a client who was picking up an order for the pet adoption center overheard me. He said he's a retired lawyer. His firm handled everything for Mr. Bowers, including his will."

Trevor ceased his pacing for a moment to look at Emily triumphantly, but it was clear to her he had more news to share. She made an impatient "go on" gesture with her hand.

"The will was, apparently, a convoluted mess. Mr. Bowers kept coming in to the law firm to change things, adding all these clauses to it, and some parts contradicted others. The lawyer in charge of it all wound up being fired after Mr. Bowers died and everyone realized how confusing it all was. Anyway, that only partly explains why it took so long for the house and its contents to be sold off. The biggest reason it took so long is because, after the twins killed each other, someone came forward, claiming to be the rightful heir to the Bowers estate."

"Who?" Emily was standing now, too.

"The son of Jerry Bowers."

15

Emily was so shocked she couldn't even think of the right response. She made several attempts to say something, then finally gave up and sat down again, her breath coming out in a rush.

"I know," Trevor said. He sat down on the side of the sofa closest to Emily's chair. "Do you think that's why Judy and Jerry were fighting? Maybe Mr. Bowers was leaning toward leaving the house to Jerry so it could stay in the Bowers family. Judy didn't have any children, so leaving the house to Jerry, who could then leave it to his son, would have been the only way to keep the house in family hands."

"Assuming Mr. Bowers even knew Jerry had a son. No one we've talked to has mentioned him, and Annie hasn't reported finding anything in her research."

"I said the same thing to the lawyer. He said Jerry had never told people he had a son—it would have been a big family scandal, I suppose—but he probably told his father about it in an effort to secure the house for himself. When the son showed up at the law office to claim the inheritance he thought he was owed, he was explicit about keeping it a secret until the estate was settled in his favor."

"Except it wasn't settled in his favor, and the house was sold. I wonder why?"

"Because the man was claiming to be Jerry's son, but

he was nowhere to be found in Jerry's will. He wasn't able to legally prove Jerry was his father, either."

"Wow. No wonder Judy and Jerry were fighting all the time. It also helps explain why Jerry was more interested in simply owning the house, as opposed to Judy's plans to profit off the land. She was going to build condos on that lot."

Trevor laughed. "And my dad's construction company probably would have built them, even though condos would stick out like a sore thumb in that neighborhood."

"It sounds like this scandal goes beyond just two siblings who didn't like each other. Apparently, Mr. Bowers was fairly well-respected around town. It's a shame his kids didn't take after him."

"Now that I've shared my big news, I'm heading home." Trevor stood and stretched.

"You're welcome to stay for dinner," Emily said, surprised Trevor was leaving so soon. "After all, you drove all the way out here."

"Thanks, but I've actually got plans later tonight. Hopefully, there are no ghosts and no scandals at the movie theater! Let me know if you learn anything new this weekend."

"I will. Thank you, Trevor. Have a nice night." Emily walked Trevor out the front door, turning left on the front porch as he headed toward his car. She gazed at Hilltop Cemetery, now full of shadows as twilight deepened. It was still warm out, but it would likely be a nice temperature for ghost hunting later in the evening. Emily made a mental note to take a can of bug spray with her.

The evening passed swiftly. Trish stopped by not long after Trevor had left, armed with baked goods and the latest gossip. Emily's guests drove to a restaurant for dinner, leaving her to cook and eat by herself. Still, it seemed like only a short time before they returned.

Clearly, they were eager to start their investigation in the cemetery.

Emily led the group through Hilltop's iron gate, but not before warning them to look out for roots and uneven spots in the brick paths. Now that the sun was down, the cemetery seemed especially dark, as if the shadows were thickening under the oak and magnolia trees.

They were halfway up the hill before Hal suddenly groaned. "I left my tape recorder on the dining room table! Can I go back?"

"Of course," Emily said, fishing her keys out of her pocket and handing them over. "Just lock up behind yourself when you're done. When you get back, turn left when you reach the fourth ring path."

Based on Emily's information about the cemetery, Catherine had decided the group should start their investigation at the Dawson mausoleum, where the resident patriarch was known to get flirtatious with women from time to time.

In all, the investigation was a quiet one. Emily used the time to sit a short distance away from the group, trying to sense anything paranormal around her. With her eyes closed, Emily whispered an invitation for any spirits present to come talk to her, then sat as still as possible as she listened for any response.

She didn't hear or feel a thing.

After the ghost hunters called it a night shortly after one o'clock in the morning, Emily trudged back to the house, feeling exhausted and disappointed. She fervently hoped her guests would find something on their recordings because their night had been uneventful, too.

It wasn't until Emily got closer to the house that she realized how dark it was. Her feet were moving her along the path she knew so well, so she hadn't really been paying attention to the scene in front of her. At first, she simply thought she had forgotten to turn on the porch light. She was surprised that not a single light inside the house was on, either, since she thought she remembered leaving the parlor lights on when they all headed to the cemetery.

When they reached the front door, Emily went in and flicked the switch for the hall light. Nothing happened. It was the same in the parlor. "The power's off," she said, turning to look over the heads of her guests, who were still filing in through the door. Beyond the porch and the driveway, the street light closest to the house was shining a pale yellow. That meant the power was only off at Eternal Rest.

With a sigh, Emily fished her flashlight out of her pocket. Occasions like this were rare. Usually, the power at the house only went off if there was a bad storm. "Hang on, y'all. I'm going to check the fuses."

Emily went out the back door, down the steps, and turned left to face the storm cellar. She hated going down there. There was just something about basements Emily didn't like, and they always gave her a claustrophobic feeling. She especially didn't want to go down there with nothing but a flashlight.

"Silly," Emily said to herself. "It's not even haunted down there, so why are you being such a wimp? Nothing is going to happen."

Steeling herself, Emily swung open the doors and plunged into the dark cellar. She found her way to the fuse box, and, sure enough, the main fuse for the house had been tripped. She wasn't sure what could have overloaded it, but she quickly flipped the switch. Soft light suddenly lit up the top of the cellar steps, and Emily knew the back porch light had come on again. Satisfied, she turned off her flashlight and mentally congratulated herself on tackling the dark cellar alone.

Emily walked in the back door and headed straight for the kitchen to make coffee for the next day, noticing the house was once again ablaze with light. Normally, she would have taken care of prepping the coffee before escorting guests to the cemetery, but between Trevor's news and her own thoughts about the Bowers twins, it had completely slipped her mind.

Emily didn't realize anything was amiss until she heard Catherine shout. A moment later, Blake appeared in the kitchen doorway. Emily was already heading toward the hallway to find out what had prompted the outburst, and she ran right into Blake. "Oh, sorry! Is everything okay?" Emily already knew the answer to her question. Blake's expression showed that everything was definitely not okay.

"It's all gone," he said in a rush.

"What is?"

"The research."

Emily narrowed her eyes, trying to understand. "What do you mean it's gone?"

Blake took Emily gently by the arm and steered her toward the dining room, where the ghost hunters had left their laptops, headphones, and other gear. He walked quickly while saying, "All of the notes we've written down are just gone. They were on the table, and now they're not."

When Emily walked into the dining room, the first thing she noticed was the dismayed look on Annie's face. "My notebook!" she cried. "It's just... gone!"

"My notes are missing, too," Catherine said.

"Okay," Emily said in a calming voice. "Are you sure you left them here on the table? Maybe they're upstairs in your rooms, or in the parlor."

"They're not," Catherine insisted.

"We should look, just to make sure," Blake said, glancing at his girlfriend. "I'll go check. Andy, why don't you come up with me, and we can look in your room, too?"

As the two men headed upstairs, Emily looked around at the others. "Is anything else missing?"

Hal was sorting through a stack of memory cards and USB sticks. "My things are all here. Why would someone break in and take only our notes? Why not grab our laptops, too?"

"Don't jump to conclusions," Emily warned. "We don't even know if the notes are really missing or just misplaced. And if they are missing, it could just as easily have been a ghost hiding things away."

"That would mean Judy Bowers took them," Catherine said. "Why would she want to steal our notes?"

Before Emily could find an answer to that question, Blake and Andy returned. They reported there were no notes upstairs. The research really was missing.

Hal looked pointedly at Emily. "Judy's ghost hasn't been moving objects, and as far as we know, she can't even get out of the mirror. I know you don't want to think someone broke into your house, Emily, but that's the most likely explanation."

"But, as you already said, why would someone break in just to take notes? There's a small fortune in computers sitting right here." Emily really didn't want to think of someone sneaking into her house and stealing things, all while she and her guests were just a few hundred yards away, with the house in their line of sight. She really, really hoped it was a ghost who had taken them for some reason. Ghosts had moved objects in her home before, so why not now?

Emily realized all her guests were staring at her, and she sighed. "I'll call the police tomorrow, but I don't know that they'll be able to find anything helpful." With a self-conscious laugh, Emily put her hand to her forehead. "I have security cameras! Let's check those."

It wasn't until Emily sat down at her desk and pulled

up the security company's website that she realized the futility of the task. The power had been off, so the cameras hadn't been working. Still, she logged into her account and looked at the footage from the front and back door cameras. They went dark just after midnight, long after she and her guests had gone to the cemetery. If someone had broken into her house, it was possible they had gone into the storm cellar first and flipped the fuse to disable the cameras.

Emily relayed this thought to her guests, then added, "What I don't understand is why neither door looks disturbed. No broken locks, no broken windows. How did they get in?"

"Oh, no," Hal said softly. His cheeks turned scarlet, and he buried his face in his hands. "After I got my tape recorder, I probably forgot to lock the door. I am so sorry."

Emily shook her head. "No, I unlocked the door when we got back. I would have noticed if it wasn't locked to begin with."

"Maybe…" Andy began. He frowned, then held his hands out, palms up. His left hand dipped as he said, "Maybe the intruder locked the door on their way out, not thinking about the fact they had found it open." Andy's other hand lowered. "Or, maybe it was a ghost, and no one broke in."

Emily looked around the room, trying to spot any little differences, but everything was in place. "Unfortunately, I don't think that's something we're going to be able to figure out tonight. Let's all go to bed, and maybe we'll get some answers tomorrow morning, when our brains are a little more fresh."

Everyone reluctantly agreed, and Emily could perfectly understand the nervous look on Annie's face. She felt the same. Once her guests were in their rooms, Emily made a complete circuit of the downstairs, checking every door and window to ensure they were all closed and locked. She pulled curtains tightly shut and left lights on in both the parlor and the dining room.

Finally finished, Emily was walking toward her bedroom and wondering how in the world she was going to be able to fall asleep when there was a quiet knock on the front door. She froze, instantly afraid. Who would be knocking on her front door at nearly two o'clock in the morning? Emily had the sudden, irrational thought that someone had, indeed, broken in earlier, and they were now back for more.

Emily silently berated herself for such a silly thought as she tiptoed to the door. She peered through the peephole and was surprised to see Reed standing there. Emily threw open the door. Reed was glancing nervously over his shoulder, and when he turned his face to Emily's, she gasped. She was used to Reed being the stoic one, the kind of person who could experience something paranormal without ever sounding excited or nervous about it. Now, though, he was almost twitchy, his right thumb rubbing his left palm and his weight constantly shifting from one leg to the other.

As she pulled him inside and quickly shut and locked the door, Emily noticed Reed was wearing a T-shirt and pajama pants. She would have laughed if the situation had been different.

"Emily," Reed said gravely, "something strange is going on."

16

Reed cleared his throat and straightened his shoulders. When he spoke again, he sounded more like the calm, collected friend Emily was used to. "I'm glad you're still up. I figured your guests were going to do some ghost hunting, so I hoped I might catch you before you went to bed. First of all, are you okay?"

"Funny you should ask that." Emily led Reed into the parlor and pointed to the sofa as she settled into a chair. "The theme of this week seems to be 'something weird just happened,' because it's true for us, too." Emily told Reed about the missing research notes and the mysterious power outage, and he nodded grimly as she finished.

"Have you felt like you're being watched?" he asked.

"Not just me. Annie—she's one of my guests—felt that way at the library, and Sage called earlier to say she was closing her shop and heading home early because she kept getting the same sensation."

"You can add me to the list. I went to bed at my usual time, but I woke up around half past one." Reed leaned forward and propped his elbows on his knees. "I thought I'd heard a noise, like a bang. I didn't hear anything else, but just to be sure, I got up and looked outside. I would swear there was something out there, in the dark."

"Or someone," Emily said. "I hate the idea that

someone broke in here, but it seems more likely than a ghost stopping by to take a few things."

There was a creak on the stairs, and both Emily's and Reed's eyes shot to the parlor doorway. Hal soon appeared, still dressed and looking like he wasn't even tired. "You okay, Emily?"

"I'm fine. You remember Reed? He's been getting that watchful feeling, too." Emily turned her attention to Reed again. "And if you heard a banging noise, it's possible someone was doing more than watching. Have you checked to see if your house has any signs of an attempted break-in?"

"I haven't checked, but I will, in the daylight. If someone came here to steal research notes and followed your guest at the library, then clearly there is more to the Bowers twins' murders than we thought. Somebody doesn't want you knowing something."

"Maybe somebody doesn't want us to know about Jerry's son," Emily mused.

When Reed expressed his surprise, Emily realized he wasn't caught up on the latest news from Trevor. When she finished telling him, he sat back and gazed at the ceiling thoughtfully. "That makes sense," he said, "except for one thing: why would anyone connected to that family be shadowing me and Sage? We certainly don't have any secret information."

"I wish I knew, Reed." Emily paused, then added, "So, we definitely think it must be a person and not a ghost causing trouble?" Emily was still clinging to the hope that the strange feelings and events were simply some kind of spectral shenanigans.

Reed just looked at Emily, his eyebrows raised.

"I know," she said in a defeated tone. "That theory would make sense if the weird stuff was only happening here, but it's happening all over the place."

"Do you think we're in danger?" Hal asked. He was still in the doorway, leaning against the frame at an angle that gave him a clear view of the front door. "Do we need to, I don't know, set a watch, or something?"

"There are currently seven of us in this house. Anyone, ghost or living, would be foolish to break in here right now. Reed, why don't you stay? One of my guest rooms is free, so you can go get some sleep."

When Reed tried to protest, Emily held up a hand to stop him. "I'm not letting you go home, by yourself, when we don't know what's going on. I'll feel better knowing you're here with us."

Reed reluctantly agreed, saying he didn't want to inconvenience Emily, but she brushed off his excuses. "Everyone will have to fight over the cheddar bagels in the morning, but that's as bad as it will get," she assured him. She retrieved the key for the empty room from her desk and handed it over. "I'll have breakfast ready at ten. Good night."

Emily kept her bedroom door open that night, feeling like she didn't want the extra barrier separating her from her guests. If Reed hadn't shown up, she probably would have slept in the empty room herself so all of them were together on the second floor. She felt isolated down on the ground floor, especially with the back door so close to her bedroom door.

Sleep didn't come for a long time. Even after she drifted off, Emily woke up time and time again during the night, until her curtains began to glow in the early sun. Knowing it was daylight finally calmed her nerves, and she slept soundly until her alarm told her it was time to get up and prepare breakfast.

Emily was putting breakfast on the sideboard in the dining room as Andy and Annie wandered in, yawning. "Good morning!" Emily said as brightly as she could.

"Morning," Andy mumbled. He poured coffee for himself and Annie, and the two of them sank down into chairs. Emily guessed they had spent a troubled night, as well.

Reed came in next, looking like he had slept much better than Andy and Annie. Emily was about to ask him how he had enjoyed his room when her phone rang. It was Sage's name on the screen, and Emily had a sinking feeling as she answered. Somehow, she knew Sage was calling with bad news.

"Em, you need to get to my shop, right now." Sage's voice was tight.

"Are you okay?" *How many times are we all going to have to ask each other that?*

"I'm fine. But you need to get here immediately, and then we're going to the police station. I'll see you in ten minutes!" With that, Sage hung up the phone.

"Sage wants me to go to her shop, though she wouldn't say why," Emily said, looking at Reed. "Can you please keep an eye on things here while I run over there?"

"You got it," Reed promised, talking around a big bite of croissant.

Emily snatched up a bagel before dashing to her bedroom to grab her purse. She was pulling out of her driveway in less than a minute, and as she drove, grabbing bites of her bagel when she could, she reminded herself to stick to the speed limit. Whatever was happening at Sage's shop, it wasn't worth getting a speeding ticket for.

The Art Deco office building where Seeing Beyond was located sat two streets away from the square in downtown Oak Hill. It was quiet since it was a Saturday: Sage owned one of the few businesses in the building that was open on the weekends. Emily raced up the stairs to the second floor and swung open the door of Seeing Beyond. She stopped, looking around for a sign that things were amiss. She saw nothing, but she did hear Sage's low voice speaking behind a curtained-off area between tall bookshelves, which created a little nook where Sage worked with her clients. Realizing Sage must have had a client scheduled for that morning, Emily forced herself to relax her shoulders since they felt like they were up around her ears.

Knowing it would be rude, not to mention unprofessional, to interrupt Sage while she was with a client, Emily sat down on the midnight-blue velvet sofa. Combined with the dark-toned throw rugs scattered everywhere and heavy drapes, the space gave off a distinct Victorian vibe despite being in a bright, modernized office space. Usually, Emily found the ambience calming. After sitting for just a few minutes, though, she was on her feet again, making a nervous circuit of the room as she took in every little detail. Still, she could find no signs that anything was wrong.

To Emily, it felt like an hour that Sage was with her client. In reality, it was only about twenty minutes before the gold brocade curtain opened and a thin, balding, middle-aged man walked out. He smiled and said good morning to Emily before thanking Sage and leaving.

"Well?" Emily prompted. She noticed that not only did Sage shut the door after her client, but she locked it, as well.

Sage waved Emily to her desk, a hulking walnut antique that sat in a corner. Wordlessly, Sage moved behind her desk, slid open a drawer, and took out a piece of paper. She handed it to Emily. The paper was brown and thick, and Emily instantly thought of a paper grocery bag. It was roughly cut into a square shape. In thick black marker, someone had written *STOP LOOKING. STOP ASKING QUESTIONS. MIND YOUR OWN BUSINESS.* The childish scrawl was in capital letters, and Emily wondered if the person who wrote it was trying to disguise their real handwriting.

"Someone slid it under my door last night," Sage explained.

Emily perched on the edge of Sage's desk, staring at the words. "Reed was right," she murmured.

"Explain," Sage said.

Sage was shocked when Emily told her about Reed's suspected visitor in the middle of the night. Like Emily, she couldn't understand why someone would target him. "I can understand why someone would threaten me," Sage said. "I'm your best friend, I can communicate with the ghost of Judy Bowers, and I'm always involved when you're trying to catch a killer. But why would someone go after Reed?"

Emily shrugged. "He was with us when we used the glass to communicate through the mirror. Maybe someone saw him go inside my house. Of course, Trevor was there, too, and he hasn't reported anything happening to him."

Sage made a noise that was somewhere between a snort and a snicker. "I like Trevor, but he's not exactly in touch with his intuition. Remember, Em, you're exploring skills most people don't even want to admit they have. Someone could be watching Trevor all day long, and he wouldn't notice."

"I hate this, Sage," Emily said honestly. "I haven't even told you the worst part, yet. Someone broke into my house last night while we were at the cemetery. They stole all the research notes my guests had on the dining room table. At first, I hoped it might be a ghost causing problems. I would have been okay with that."

"But you're not okay with a living, breathing person threatening you. I get it." Sage came around the desk so that she stood right next to Emily. Putting an arm around

Emily's shoulders, she said, "Whoever is doing this might be content just to make threats, but what if they aren't? This could get ugly really fast, and it's time to go to the police."

"You're right." Emily leaned into Sage, feeling deflated. "Why did I have to buy that stupid mirror?"

"Oh, come on. You like helping ghosts. Maybe you were meant to buy that mirror. If it had gone to anyone else, they might have ignored the haunting, or taken measures to banish the ghost instead of helping it."

"From everything I've heard about the Bowers twins, I'm not even sure I want to help Judy."

Sage clicked her tongue impatiently. "You've helped jerk ghosts before. Why stop now?"

"I don't enjoy the feeling that I'm possibly putting my life or my home in danger to do so. Remember, trying to help the ghost of Robert Gaines nearly got me poisoned."

"So, don't accept a drink from anyone who's a suspect."

Emily gave Sage a smile. Her friend's practicality was almost funny in this situation, but she knew Sage wanted to get answers as much as she did. "I'll call Detective Hernandez and tell him everything."

"No, you won't," Sage said. "You and I are walking to the police station right now. If anyone is outside watching my building, I want them to see us go there. In fact, I actually hope they're watching us right now. I want them to know that we aren't hesitating to go to the authorities. They wanted to scare us with this note, and we're going to scare them by bringing in the police."

The police station was only a few blocks away. The late morning sunshine was already hot, and Emily could feel a bead of sweat along her forehead. Still, something about being out on the sidewalk in the glaring light of day was comforting. It felt safer than being at home.

When Sage and Emily walked through the front door of the historic brick building that was the Oak Hill Police Department, the first person they saw was Roger Newton. He was walking right toward them, his close-cropped blond hair looking even more gray at the temples. He stalked right up to Emily, shaking his head. "Miss Emily, what now? Do you have another dead body on your hands?"

"Hi, Roger. Er, Officer Newton." Emily flashed her most charming smile at him. She liked Roger, but he always seemed to assume she was getting into trouble of some sort. Given their history with each other, it was easy to see why he felt that way, but it still irked Emily. "No dead bodies today. Someone broke into my house last night."

Roger's expression quickly changed from disapproval to concern. "Are you okay? Was anything valuable taken?"

"Nothing of worth, no. And yes, I'm fine, as are my guests. We were hoping Detective Hernandez might be around so we can give him the details. Unfortunately, Sage had a problem at her shop, and we think the two incidents are related."

"Come on, I'll take you back to his office. You're lucky. He's not usually here on Saturdays. Neither am I, for that matter."

"What brings you in today, then?"

"Thieves were apparently busy last night. It wasn't just your house that got broken into. Someone also broke into the library. Of all places! What are they going to steal? A book they could check out for free?"

Emily stopped, and Roger took a few steps before he realized Emily was no longer behind him. "Miss Emily?"

"Newspapers," Emily said. "I'll bet you anything they took the microfiche files with the articles about the Bowers twins' murders."

17

Roger's eyes narrowed, his disapproving look back in full force. He crossed his arms over his stocky chest as he said sourly, "So this *is* about a murder."

"Apparently. All because I bought one haunted mirror for a guest bedroom."

Emily could almost feel Roger's change of mood. He was a die-hard skeptic, even though he had experienced several paranormal things while with Emily.

"You should join us in Hernandez's office," Sage suggested. "Ghost or not, there are some concerning things going on with the living. We can use all the help we can get."

That seemed to appease Roger, and he relaxed his arms. Still, there was an edge to his voice when he spoke again, as if he were dealing with children telling wild stories. "Come on, then." He turned and continued on to an office at the back of the building.

Unlike Roger, Danny Hernandez seemed happy to see Emily and Sage. "Hello, ladies," he said brightly. "To what do I owe the pleasure?"

"Nothing pleasant," Sage countered. She pulled the note she had received from her purse and plunked it down in front of Danny.

Danny's lips moved as he read the note to himself, then

he looked up at Sage, the concern clear in his eyes. "Someone left this for you?"

"Yes. They slid it under the door of my office."

"Do you have any idea what they're talking about?"

Sage looked at Emily and gave her a little nod, prompting her to unfold the story. Emily started at the very beginning, with the mirror. She hadn't gotten very far when Danny stopped her to retrieve a notebook and pen. "Okay, go on," he said, his pen poised above his paper.

Emily caught the way Roger rolled his eyes as she described the screeching and shouting coming from the mirror, but he turned serious again when she got to the part about the break-in.

"And now, Roger says the library was broken into," Emily continued. "Two of my guests went there to do research, pulling everything they could find about the Bowers twins from old newspaper articles on microfiche. That's the information that was stolen from my house."

Danny was nodding, his pen still flying across the paper. "So maybe they took the files so you can't go back and look again." He flipped to a new page and wrote in large letters: *Who? Why?*

Roger cleared his throat. "You know I don't believe in ghosts," he said, "but I do believe you two might be in real danger. I'm not scheduled to work this weekend, but I'm going to be making rounds of both your houses. As a friend, not as a police officer. I'm going to give you my cell phone number before you leave here. I'm available any time."

This time, when Emily smiled at Roger, it wasn't in an attempt to be charming. It was a genuine smile of gratitude. He might be impatient with her talk of ghosts, but it was nice to know Roger thought of himself as a friend. Emily decided she liked that very much.

Danny ordered both Sage and Emily to lay low for the rest of the day. "I don't want you doing more research, I don't want you talking to any more neighbors, and I definitely don't want you out wandering the cemetery alone," he told them firmly.

"Do you really think it's that bad?" Emily asked.

"I hope it's not, but I'd like to err on the side of caution here."

Sage had more clients scheduled for the afternoon, but she promised to be on the lookout and to call if anything odd happened. Emily needed to get back to Eternal Rest to check in on her guests and to do some cleaning. Satisfied with their respective plans, Danny sent them on their way while Roger promised he would be patrolling that night.

Emily walked back to Seeing Beyond with Sage, feeling reluctant to leave her best friend alone. "I'll be fine," Sage assured. "I'll even text Jen and ask her to come sit with me. She can bring a book and chill on the sofa."

Satisfied with that answer, Emily left, driving back to Eternal Rest with the calming knowledge that the police were on the case.

Emily passed on the warnings Hernandez had given her and Sage, telling her guests they should probably steer away from anything having to do with the Bowers twins. Catherine readily agreed, especially since Annie had gone pale when she learned the library had been broken into. The five of them would, Catherine assured Emily, go two towns over to visit a few haunted spots there. "None of the ghosts we meet today will have ever even heard of the Bowers twins!" Catherine said confidently.

With her guests gone, Emily was able to clean the rooms and eat lunch at her leisure. She heard shouting from upstairs as she bit into a turkey sandwich, but now that she knew it was just Judy Bowers hollering, she didn't feel at all unnerved by it. She did still wonder why Judy seemed so upset and how her shouting tied in to the strange activity happening among the living.

At two o'clock, Emily stretched out on the sofa, ready to take a short nap. Her house was quiet, her work was done, and she didn't feel like unseen eyes were staring at her.

At ten minutes past two, the doorbell rang. Emily grumbled all the way to the door, until her annoyance turned into curiosity as she looked through the peephole and saw Trish. She swung open the door and saw how nervous Trish looked. Her petite body almost seemed to be vibrating.

"What's going on?" Emily asked, worried Trish would report feeling watched, too.

Instead, Trish answered in rapid-fire delivery, "Emily, you won't believe what happened to me today! Actually, you will. My aunt was in town last weekend, and she visited a couple of the local antique shops. She gave me a pretty little handheld mirror that she found. She said it would look great in the bakery's bathroom. You know I have it decorated like an old-fashioned powder room. Anyway, I was all alone in the bakery today, and I started hearing this yelling. It was like someone was standing outside my front door, shouting through the glass. There was no one outside on the side-walk, but I kept hearing the shouting. It was coming from the bathroom, Emily! I think that mirror is haunted!"

Trish stopped to catch her breath. Her eyes had gotten wider as she continued talking, and now she looked almost comical.

"Do you have it with you?" Emily asked.

"It's in my car."

"Do you know where the mirror came from? That's so similar to what's going on in my mirror!"

Trish nodded triumphantly. "It came from the Bowers estate. I called my aunt to find out where she'd bought it, then I called Everything Old is New Again to find out where they'd bought it, and then I called old Mrs. Greene to find out where *she* had bought it. Her son had to be our go-between. That poor old lady can't hear for anything, but she was shocked that I was the second person to contact her about a haunted mirror. It must have been in the room where those twins killed each other."

Emily felt like she needed to sit down she was so surprised by Trish's story, but she settled for steadying herself against the doorframe. "That mirror was probably on a dresser or vanity in the bedroom where they killed each other. I've got Judy Bowers upstairs in my mirror. I'm guessing you have Jerry Bowers in yours. Each twin's spirit must have gotten trapped in a mirror. Or they chose to go into the mirrors instead of crossing over." Emily had a sudden, ridiculous thought, and she laughed. "Maybe they wanted to keep fighting with each other, even after death!"

Trish's line of thinking was much more practical. "What do we do?"

"My ghost hunters aren't here right now, so we'll call Sage. Bring the mirror inside!"

Emily's call to Sage went straight to voicemail, and she left a message, knowing Sage must be with one of her afternoon clients. In the meantime, Emily and Trish sat in the parlor, each armed with a glass of sweet tea. The hand-held mirror, which was made of silver and had an ornate *B* engraved on the back, was sitting across the hall on the dining room table. After showing it to Emily, Trish had rewrapped it in a dish towel from the bakery. She said she knew a towel couldn't stop a ghost, but she felt like it was watching her if she didn't cover it up.

"This might answer a mystery," Trish said. "Earlier this week, when I was here, you remember I got that call from my security company? A motion detector inside the bakery was going off, but neither of the door alarms had been tripped. When I went to check it out, everything was locked up tight, and nothing was disturbed. Nothing, that is, except that mirror."

"Really?" Emily's eyes turned upward, to the spot where her full-length mirror was sitting above them. "Mine doesn't do anything."

"I left the mirror on the side table in the bathroom. I swear I did," Trish said. "When I got to the bakery, it was sitting on the countertop next to the cash register. At the time, I brushed it off as me having a bad memory. I also considered that a customer had moved it there, and I just hadn't noticed. Now, I'm almost certain it's what set off the motion detector."

"I'm impressed Jerry has learned how to drive the mirror around," Emily said. At the same time, she was relieved her own mirror wasn't moving on its own. That might be a little too creepy, even for her.

Trish shifted gears to talking about how busy she had been, telling Emily that if things kept going the way they were, she would have a record summer. Emily was only half listening, her mind still focused on the ghosts of Judy and Jerry Bowers, when the doorbell rang.

When Emily answered the door, she saw Sage standing there, breathless. "I got your voicemail," she gasped. "Where's Jerry?"

Sage made a beeline for the mirror, seeming to know exactly where it was even before Emily told her, and brought it into the parlor. She removed the towel with a flourish and held it up. "Hello, Jerry Bowers!" she said enthusiastically. "I am so glad you've joined us! Let's get started!"

"I grabbed an empty glass when I got tea for me and Trish," Emily said. She picked it up off her desk and handed it to Sage. "Do you think we need a tape recorder?"

"For sure. Jerry will probably be speaking backward, just like Judy. Where's Hal?"

"Gone for the day. I can use my phone to record the conversation, though."

Sage agreed, but the disappointment in her voice was clear. "Okay, but then we'll have to wait for Hal to get back so he can reverse the audio. Unless you have software on your laptop that can do it?"

"I don't," Emily said reluctantly.

"I can actually help there," Trish said. "Clint has been driving me nuts since we got him some kind of music software for his birthday. He thinks he's making music, but it just sounds like loud noise to me. Still, I bet he can flip a recording for us. I'll text him right now and tell him to bring his laptop over."

Satisfied, Sage held the glass up against the small mirror as Emily started the recording app on her cell phone. "Hello, Jerry," Sage called again, but this time, her voice was lower, more monotone. Emily knew she had shifted into spirit communication mode. "Jerry, your sister Judy is here, too. Do you have a message for her?" After a long pause, Sage continued, "Do you know your spirit is trapped in a mirror?"

Sage continued to ask questions, though there were no answers to actually hear. Just as she called a halt to the interview, Clint arrived. Emily let him in and was surprised to see how much more grown-up he looked than the last time she had seen him. His once-shaggy light-brown hair was now neatly trimmed, and his gangly limbs had filled out. Even though he was dressed in a threadbare T-shirt and faded jeans, Emily could see how he might be a good assistant for her. With the right clothes, he would look fairly professional.

Clint walked into the parlor slowly, his eyes constantly darting around the room. Emily suspected Trish had told him why she needed his help, and he was on the lookout for ghosts. She put a hand on his shoulder to steer him toward the sofa while saying, "It's okay. You're not actually going to see a ghost." She could feel the way his muscles relaxed at the words.

In short order, Clint had fired up the music program on his laptop and retrieved Emily's recording from her phone. He hit a few buttons, then said proudly, "This should do it!"

The four of them sat, eyes on the laptop, and listened. Sage's voice could be heard from time to time, but it was backward since the recording had been reversed. After ten minutes of no answering voice, Emily was beginning to give up hope when a man's voice suddenly growled, "He killed me!"

18

"Wow!" Clint said. "That's a real ghost!"

"It is," Trish said. "Great work, Clint! And great work, Sage!"

Emily and Sage simply looked at each other, shocked. "But... That's not right," Emily finally said.

Sage continued staring at Emily while she said, "Clint, can you please play that again?"

Once again, the four of them heard the voice say, "He killed me."

"Jerry is definitely saying 'he.'" Emily stood and began pacing in the spot where Trevor had been doing the same, only the day before.

"But his sister killed him," Trish said. "Everyone knows the twins killed each other."

"Maybe that's why they're both haunting mirrors. What everyone thinks is the truth is wrong." Emily gave a half-hearted laugh. "Why does a haunting at Eternal Rest always turn into finding a murderer?"

"Consider it a privilege, Em," Sage said, clearly undaunted by the idea. "It's a chance for you to help ghosts get justice."

Emily remembered Trevor had once said essentially the same thing to her, and she shrugged. "You're right. Let's listen to the rest of the tape to see if Jerry has any more surprises for us."

He didn't. The rest of the recording was just silence and Sage's backward questions.

By the time the recording was done, Sage was already picking up the mirror and the glass. "We're not doing this very efficiently," she said, moving toward the hall. "Let's go upstairs and talk to both ghosts at once! I'm sure your guests won't mind us being in their room for this."

Emily thought Sage was right about that, but just in case, she called the phone number in the group's reservation. It was Catherine who answered, and when Emily explained the situation, she was more than amenable to the idea. "That's amazing!" Catherine shouted as Emily held the phone away from her ear. "The other twin is there, too? Wow, we're going to come back early so we can also try talking to Jerry!"

"That's a yes from Catherine," Emily said after the call ended.

"I assumed so," Sage said, smiling. "Let's go! I'm stopping in the kitchen first for another glass!"

Soon, Emily had led Sage, Trish, and Clint to Jaxon's room. Emily and Sage sat on the rug in front of the floor mirror while Trish and Clint settled on the foot of the bed. Emily started the recording, then held one of the glasses against the full-length mirror. Sage held the other against the handheld mirror.

"Jerry and Judy, I bet it's been a long time since you were both in the same room at the same time," Sage began. "Jerry, is there anything you want to say to your twin sister? Judy, do you have a message for Jerry?"

From there, Sage began asking more pointed questions, like who each one was talking about when they said "he" had killed them. She asked about any enemies they had, and whether anyone was trying to take their inheritance away from them.

"Oh, ask about Jerry's son!" Emily said.

"Jerry, why did you keep the fact that you have a son a secret?" Sage asked. "Did you have a good relationship with him? Did you want him to inherit the Bowers mansion when you died?"

As soon as Sage ended her last question, a high-pitched screeching noise sounded so loudly everyone jerked backward and clamped their hands over their ears. Emily nearly dropped her glass in her effort to drown out the noise.

Once it was silent again, Emily tentatively lowered her hands. "That came from the big mirror," she said.

"It sounded like nails on a chalkboard," Trish said, her voice oddly pitched.

"Or nails on the backside of a mirror," Emily amended.

"I think," Sage said, gazing at the full-length mirror, "that Judy Bowers didn't know about her nephew. Either that, or she didn't like him for some reason."

"I have a feeling that if Judy could get out of her mirror, she'd smash the one Jerry's in without a second thought. That sounded angry." Emily's eyes were actually turned to the handheld mirror, her hands still hovering about shoulder-height. She was expecting Jerry to respond, and she was worried the sound would be equally loud. "Do you think Jerry's son could be the one who murdered the twins? That could explain why Judy got so upset just now."

"Let's ask!" Sage said. She picked up her glass and indicated Emily should do the same. "Judy, did Jerry's son kill you?"

There was only silence this time, and Emily breathed a sigh of relief when the scratching noise didn't return. Sage tried asking the question several different ways before moving on to other questions.

There were no more noises, and Emily could only hope that when Clint reversed the recording, they would hear some answers.

Clint was working on doing just that when Emily's guests returned. He was sitting at the dining room table with his laptop while Emily, Sage, and Trish sat watching him expectantly.

"We sped all the way back here," Catherine announced proudly. "What have we missed?"

"Jerry Bowers, who's in the small mirror, is saying the same thing as his sister: 'He killed me,'" Emily explained. "Everyone has always thought the twins killed each other, but according to Jerry, that's not correct. The question, then, is who did actually kill them?"

"Also," Sage interjected, "Judy did not like it when we brought up the subject of Jerry's son."

Clint cleared his throat. "I'm ready when you are."

Everyone fell silent to listen to the recording. Emily had lost track of the time up in the room, and she was surprised at how long she had been documenting the question and answer session. They listened for what seemed like hours, and Emily actually caught herself yawning from boredom. Jerry and Judy had both remained stubbornly silent, and everyone expressed disappointment when the recording finally ended without yielding any answers.

"We'll keep trying," Catherine said, but even her usual firmness was tinged with doubt.

"I'll help you, if that's okay," Sage said.

Catherine readily agreed. As Sage and the ghost hunters prepared to go upstairs again, Trish gave Emily an apologetic smile. "Now that your audio guy is back, we're going to head home," she said. "You know I believe in ghosts, Emily, but this has been a lot to take in today. I need a hot shower and a glass of wine."

"Thanks for all your help, Trish. You, too, Clint!" Emily saw them out, then realized as she shut the door that she was the only one left downstairs. She considered joining the others for the next round of questioning, but what she really wanted to do was find out who Jerry's son was and whether or not he was still in Oak Hill.

Just as she was wondering where to even begin trying to track down someone who had worked so hard to remain anonymous, Annie came bounding down the stairs. It was the first time, Emily realized, she had seen the young woman looking so energetic since the initial scare with the mirror. "Oh, Emily! I meant to tell you!" she began enthusiastically. "I found a little piece of research in my purse today! I'd wanted to jot down one last bit of information when we were at the library, but Andy was writing some things down in my notebook from a different article, so I just scribbled on the back of a receipt. Since I had forgotten all about it, I never took it out of my purse, which means whoever broke in here didn't steal it."

Holding up her chin proudly, Annie flourished a drug store receipt. Emily eagerly took it and looked at the note. *Dawes Gibson, assistant to the Bowers family*, it read. Emily frowned at the little piece of paper. "Dawes? The neighbors called him Wes."

Annie shrugged. "A nickname, probably."

"Probably," Emily said slowly as she thought back. "Let's check the phone book! There wasn't a Wesley Gibson listed, but I seem to remember a Dawes."

Emily's memory had been correct. Dawes Gibson was listed at an address just a few blocks north of downtown Oak Hill. "Thank you, Annie! This is so helpful!" Emily immediately hurried out of the parlor and up the stairs. She didn't even stop to think about the fact that Sage and her guests were trying to have an EVP session with the Bowers ghosts. She simply barged right into the room and announced, "We have a name and an address for Mr. Bowers's assistant! I'm going to go talk to him right now!"

Sage looked up, startled. "Em," she said, "remember what Hernandez told us. We're supposed to keep to ourselves in case our mysterious stalker is watching."

Emily groaned. "Oh, yeah. I forgot."

"You could call him," Sage suggested.

"I guess." Emily knew she was pouting now, but she had been excited about the idea of learning more about the Bowers family, and trying to get Wes Gibson to open up over the phone might not be as easy as doing it in person.

"Then again," Sage continued, one corner of her mouth turning up mischievously, "you could send Trevor over there. He's eager to help out with this, and as far as we know, no one has been spying on him."

"I'd really like to do it myself, but you're right. I should stay here where I can't get in any trouble." Emily sighed. She returned to the parlor slowly. She felt like they were making progress, and she was frustrated about having to sit on the sidelines. Still, she did as Sage had suggested, calling Trevor and asking him if he'd be willing to pay Wes a visit. Trevor agreed readily, saying he would go immediately. "I'll come to Eternal Rest afterward, so I can fill you in on anything I learn in person," he promised.

While she waited, Emily opened her laptop and started searching online for anything she could find pertaining to the Bowers twins, the Bowers estate, or even to Wes Gibson. She didn't find any new information, and when the doorbell rang about an hour later, Emily crossed her fingers and hoped Trevor had had better luck than her.

Emily knew Trevor had something interesting to share the second she opened the door. He was bouncing on the balls of his feet and biting one lip anxiously. "Well?" Emily asked.

"Aren't you going to let me in?"

Emily could hear the restrained excitement in Trevor's voice. She hurriedly waved him in, and as soon as the door was shut, she said again, "Well?"

"First, I'm going to sit down, and then I'm going to start at the beginning." Trevor was clearly relishing drawing out the suspense. He walked—much too slowly, in Emily's opinion—into the parlor and dropped dramatically onto the sofa. Emily followed but remained standing, facing Trevor with her arms crossed impatiently across her chest.

"Wes Gibson died last year, but his son, Louis, lives at that address now. He said Mr. Bowers had been a wonderful employer to his father for more than thirty years, but things went south when the twins moved back home. Wes hated them. They made ridiculous demands, talked down to him, and generally acted like the entitled brats they were. He was eventually fired, right after Judy yelled at him for allowing a silver candlestick to become tarnished. The candlestick, it should be noted, was in storage in the attic and hadn't been used in years."

Emily leaned forward over the coffee table. "None of that is surprising, but it sounds like you got him to open up quite a bit."

"Oh, I did," Trevor said, smiling. "Louis told me his dad always said the absolute worst part about working there was having to perform a monthly task for Jerry. Wes had to go to the bank, withdraw two thousand dollars cash, then deliver it in an envelope to a mailbox."

"Whose mailbox was it? Why was Jerry giving someone money?" Emily gasped as a thought struck her. "Was he being blackmailed?"

"Wes wondered the same thing, so one day, he walked

right up to the house where the mailbox was and knocked on the door. The kid who answered the door was the spitting image of Jerry."

Emily's hands flew to her mouth, and she hopped from one foot to the other as she tried to hold in her excitement.

"The kid's name was Beau Greene, and Jerry was paying his mother every month to keep her mouth shut about the fact that Jerry was Beau's daddy."

Emily had the fleeting thought that she must look absolutely ridiculous. Her fingers were still pressed against her mouth, which was now open in a wide *O* of surprise. She simply stared at Trevor for a long time, too shocked to say anything. Trevor actually began to look worried, his smile of triumph turning down into a frown of concern. "Emily, are you okay?" he asked gently.

With an effort, Emily lowered her hands and forced her mouth to close. She also let out the breath she had been holding. "I don't think I am okay," she said quietly. She walked to the nearest chair and plopped down, her eyes staring at the opposite wall but not seeing it. Instead, she was picturing sweet old Stella Greene. "She's the one who bought the mirrors in the estate sale," Emily told Trevor. "Stella, Beau's mom. I met her and Beau just a few days ago!"

"I know. I recognized the name as soon as Louis Gibson said it." Trevor's smile was beginning to return.

"She never said a word about Jerry being Beau's father."

"Why would she? If it was supposed to be some big secret, then she wouldn't be likely to tell you about it."

Emily sat back and shut her eyes. She had a million questions running through her mind, and she needed a moment to quiet her brain. "Beau has been really accommodating. He let me come over to talk to his mom, and he spoke to Trish on the phone, relaying her questions to Stella," Emily said eventually. "He knew we were both looking for information on our antique mirrors, and he probably knew they came from the Bowers estate. But, if he murdered Jerry and Judy, then why has he been so willing to let us look for information?"

It was Trevor's turn to look shocked. "You think he killed the twins? Also, what does Trish have to do with this?"

"Oh, you've missed a lot! It's been a big day. Trish's aunt gave her an antique handheld mirror, and it came from the Bowers estate sale, too. Jerry is haunting that one, and he's indicated that he wasn't killed by Judy, but by some mysterious 'he.' We had a communication session with both mirrors earlier, and when Sage mentioned Jerry had a son, Judy got upset. We don't know if she was surprised to learn she had a nephew, or if she's trying to tell us he's the one who murdered them."

"So, you think whoever murdered them is the one who's been creeping around to keep an eye on you and Sage?"

"And Reed." When Trevor widened his eyes, Emily gave a short laugh. "Like I said, you've missed a lot. Frankly, I'm surprised you haven't reported feeling like you're being watched."

"I probably wouldn't notice if someone was spying on me," Trevor said frankly.

"That's just what Sage said. Anyway, Beau has been helpful, so I think it's doubtful he killed the twins."

"Emily, you know better than to trust someone just because they're acting nice." Trevor didn't need to add that his own father was a great example of that.

Emily eyed Trevor. "Want to come with me to talk to

Stella?" She knew Sage would protest, and she also knew that if Danny or Roger found out, they would give her a lecture about it. Still, Emily was too intrigued to care about following the rules at the moment. That same fierce need to show her independence was coursing through her, and she stood decisively. "I'll just pop upstairs and let Sage know we're heading out."

As Emily walked upstairs, she considered simply telling Sage she was going to run a quick errand, but she knew Sage would see right through that. Besides, Emily didn't want to lie to her best friend. Instead, she braced herself as she announced her plans.

Not surprisingly, Sage reacted like an exasperated parent. "Are you nuts? You're not supposed to be out tracking down information about the twins! I'll call Hernandez and—I don't know—ask him to put you in a jail cell overnight!"

"Don't you want to know why we're going to talk to Stella?"

Sage's eyes narrowed. "Why?"

Trevor had followed Emily upstairs, and she turned and gestured to him. "Trevor has discovered who Jerry's son is. Beau Greene is the child of Stella Greene and Jerry Bowers."

Every single person in the room started shouting at once. Finally, Emily held her hands up to quiet them down, and Trevor repeated the story he had told Emily. When he finished, Sage looked at Emily. "You want to go see Stella, knowing her son could be the killer. Her son, I should point out, who will be there with her."

"Well…" Emily felt like Sage's eyes were boring right through her.

"He wouldn't kill Emily right in front of his mom," Blake noted. He was sitting at the back of the group, and he spoke so quietly Emily almost didn't hear him.

"He's right," Catherine said, much louder than her boyfriend. "And if you flat-out ask him about being Jerry's son, you'll probably be able to tell if he's acting suspicious."

"I don't like it," Sage said, "but I can feel your determination. I'm not going to fight you on this, especially since Trevor is going with you, but I am going to call Roger and tell on you. I'll give you enough lead time to get to Stella's house, but I'm going to ask Roger to cruise past."

"Deal," Emily said. "We promise to be careful."

Trevor started to fidget as soon as he climbed into Emily's car. As she pulled out of the driveway, she glanced at him. "What is it?"

"Maybe Sage is right. Someone broke into your house, and now they're keeping tabs on all of you. This might not be a smart thing to do."

Emily had to concede Trevor was right. "I know, but I feel like we're so close to getting some answers, and I just don't want to stop now. Besides, like Blake said, Beau isn't going to do anything in front of his mother."

"No, but he, or anyone else involved in this, knows where you live. They might come after you later."

Emily frowned. "It's not that dramatic. Of course, Sage got that note, and the library was broken into—"

"What?" Trevor half turned in his seat, the seatbelt straining across his shoulder as he tried to face Emily.

"Maybe I should just start from the last time we spoke." Emily actually felt a little ashamed that she was dragging Trevor into this when he still knew so little about the threats and mysterious break-ins. She used the entire rest of the drive to Stella's house to tell Trevor everything.

As Emily pulled into the Greene family's driveway, she ended with, "Now you're up to speed."

"You do get yourself into some sticky situations, Emily."

"In my defense, all I did was buy a mirror!"

Trevor's expression turned serious as he reached over to put a hand on Emily's arm. "I will help however I can. You know that. I understand how much it means to you to help ghosts get justice, but it's not worth it if you get hurt in the process."

"I know." Emily had a moment to think Trevor was beginning to sound like Roger when she noticed Beau was standing on the front lawn, staring right at them. Emily quickly climbed out of her car and waved at him, trying to act as casually as she could despite her growing nervousness.

Am I crazy to be doing this? Am I really about to talk to the man who might have killed Judy and Jerry?

"Hi, Beau. I'm so sorry to bother you this close to dinnertime, but I was wondering if I could talk to Stella again, please? It won't take long."

Beau had been watering a flowerbed, and he gave a curt nod before turning off the spigot and coiling the hose next to it. "Mom's sure been popular this week," he said as he walked toward the door. "Come on in."

Emily and Trevor exchanged a quick glance behind Beau's back as he led the way inside the front door. Since Emily already suspected Beau, she wondered if every word he said was laced with threats or double meaning. She reminded herself, over and over, to simply relax.

Stella was in the same spot on the couch, holding a book just a few inches from her face.

"Mom!" Beau said loudly. "Emily from Eternal Rest is here again."

Stella looked up, surprised. "Oh," she simply said.

"Hi, Mrs. Greene," Emily said, matching Beau's volume. "This is my friend Trevor. Mrs. Greene, I really need your help." Emily realized that even though Beau had left the room, he could still be listening to every word she was saying. In fact, as loudly as she had to talk for Stella to hear her, Beau was probably catching the conversation without even trying. "Why don't we go sit outside? It's such a nice evening."

Stella's face took on a pinched expression briefly, but she nodded. "Help me up, young man," she said as she raised a hand toward Trevor. He helped lever her up off the sofa, and she slowly shuffled to the spacious, screened-in back porch. She and Emily sat down in the white wicker rocking chairs that overlooked the backyard while Trevor leaned against a porch column.

When Stella waved an arm toward Emily, she took that as her cue to continue. She leaned toward Stella so she could lower her voice a bit. "Stella, we have reason to believe the Bowers twins didn't kill each other."

Stella had tilted her head down so one ear was pointed toward Emily, but her head whipped up with a speed that was surprising. "Do you think they were murdered by someone else?"

Emily nodded. "We think a man killed them. Both of their ghosts have been communicating with us, saying, 'He killed me.' Stella, do you know anyone who would want to kill them?"

Stella made a noise that might have been an incredulous laugh, though it almost sounded like a choked cry. "No one liked them. I could name a dozen people who would have had reason to kill them. The man who ran the Bowers estate, Mr. Wes. Probably even old Mr. Bowers himself."

"You knew Wes Gibson?"

"Of course I did." Stella's chest rose and fell several times, and Emily saw a tear slide down one cheek. "I know why you're here. Either you figured it out, or someone told you."

"I came because I wanted to ask you if it's true that Beau is Jerry's son."

This time Stella did laugh, but it was sad. "As soon as you walked in the door, I knew you knew. Why else would you have come back? You didn't need to drag me out here to talk, though. Beau is well aware who his father is."

"Why did you keep it secret?" Emily asked, trying to inject as much kindness into the question as possible.

"Oh, my dear, it would have been such a scandal. Believe it or not, I used to be friends with Judy. Yes, she was a spoiled little princess, but with her as a friend, a whole world of opportunity opened up for me. We went horseback riding, we went out on the lake on her family's boat, we even spent weekends at fancy hotels in Atlanta! As long as I put up with her bad behavior, I got to do things a girl of my humble social standing could never have done." Stella paused, her face turned toward the lawn and her eyes unfocused.

Emily prompted, "Is that how you wound up dating Jerry?"

"Dating? Goodness, no. Jerry would have never dated a girl like me. Only rich girls for him, thank you very much. After college, we all wound up back in Oak Hill, though, and honestly, I think we were both just bored. Bored, and maybe a little nostalgic for those days when we could all romp around the Bowers estate without a care in the world. When I told him later that I was pregnant, he lost his mind. He said he would certainly never marry me, and he would never admit that any child I had was his."

"Jerk," Trevor mumbled.

"Of course, I never heard from Judy again. Jerry sent me money every month to make sure I kept my mouth shut. When it was impossible to hide my growing belly, I went down to stay at my aunt's house in Atlanta, and when I finally came back to Oak Hill a year later with a baby, I let people wonder. If anyone was ever bold enough to ask, I let them believe I'd met someone down in Atlanta. I did a good job of keeping the secret, though I think I nearly gave Mr. Wes a heart attack. He'd been delivering the money to my mailbox, but he never came up to the house. When he knocked one day, I answered the door, thinking it was my neighbor returning some tools. The poor man was so shocked when he realized what was going on. He promised to keep the secret, too, and he even helped me out in his own little way. He got Beau his first job."

"When did you tell Beau the truth?" Emily asked.

"I told him when he turned eighteen. He deserved to know. He was angry, but he went over to the Bowers mansion and spoke to Jerry. They didn't exactly have a father and son relationship, but they kept in touch. Jerry even told Beau he was changing his will so he'd inherit the mansion after he died, but he never actually did it. I don't know if he lied to Beau, or if he just didn't get around to it before—"

Stella abruptly leaned forward, her hands gripping the armrests of the rocker. "You suspect Beau, don't you? You think he killed Jerry for the house!"

"No, of course not!" Emily waved her hands to dismiss the idea, even though it was exactly what she thought.

"Beau is a good boy who loves his mama," Stella said, a fierceness in her voice that belied her frailty. "He's worked hard his whole life to build his business and to provide a good life for himself and for me. He's not greedy, and he would never kill."

"Mrs. Greene," Trevor broke in, leaving his spot by the column to come kneel in front of the old woman. "We think Mr. Bowers's will might have been a factor in the murders. Do you know anyone who would have been upset if they learned Mr. Bowers was planning to leave the house to Jerry?"

"Judy wouldn't have liked it. She was convinced she was getting the house, even before Mr. Bowers died. Mr. Wes wouldn't have been happy about it, either, since Mr. Bowers had promised him all kinds of things. I know the rumor was that Mr. Wes would get the house instead of the twins, but he said Mr. Bowers was so angry at his children that he didn't want anyone getting the house. It was supposed to be sold, along with everything in it, then razed to the ground. Mr. Wes would have gotten a big percentage of the sale as a thank you for his years of hard work."

"Do you think Wes Gibson might have murdered the twins?" Emily asked.

Stella laughed again. "No, of course not! Not that sweet old man. But I think his son might have."

20

I'm so stupid.

At the moment, it was all Emily could think. She wasn't upset with herself for not having considered that Wes Gibson or his son could be possible murderers, but because she had sent Trevor to the Gibson home without a second thought. With all the strange activity and the threat Sage had received, she hadn't stopped to think that her simple request could have had dangerous consequences for Trevor.

While Emily sat silently, Trevor said, "What makes you suspect Wes's son?"

"Mr. Wes was a sweet man, but he was bitter about those twins. You can't tell me he didn't pass that resentment on to his son. If Mr. Wes had been able to get his share of the Bowers estate, his son would have benefitted, too. You know, I bought those mirrors and a few other things at the estate sale simply because I believed Mr. Wes would eventually get the money. He outlived the twins. How about that? He got some little bit of revenge, I suppose."

"We'll ask the police to speak to Louis Gibson," Trevor assured Stella.

After that, there simply wasn't anything else to ask. Emily had more than enough to think about. As she rose and began to thank Stella, the lady took her hand and gave it a squeeze. "Can you do me a favor, Emily?"

"Yes, I'd be happy to."

"You think Jerry's ghost is haunting one of the mirrors?"

"That's right."

"I want you to give him a message for me."

"Of course. What would you like me to say?"

Stella smiled bitterly. "I want you to tell him that he's a coward and a spoiled child, and I won in the end, because I'm still alive!"

With a nervous laugh, Emily agreed to pass on the sentiments. She and Trevor helped Stella back to her spot on the couch in the living room, then said farewell.

Once Emily and Trevor were in the car, Emily said, "I'm sorry, Trevor. I put you in danger by sending you to the Gibson house. It never occurred to me that Wes Gibson might have killed the twins. And I didn't even know he had a son, let alone that the son could be a suspect, too."

"I wouldn't have gone if I thought I was really in danger."

"I don't know what's been wrong with me lately. I want to do everything myself, refusing offers of help, yet when I do finally ask for help, I wind up sending you off on a reckless adventure." Emily backed slowly out of the driveway, grateful for a reason not to look at Trevor.

"Can I be honest with you?" Trevor sounded hesitant, and Emily knew she wouldn't like whatever he was about to say, but she nodded. His voice was even quieter when he said, "I think you're becoming like a ghost."

Emily's eyes flicked toward Trevor, wondering if he was joking. His expression, though, was not only serious but sympathetic. "What do you mean?"

"You have unfinished business. Just like Scott, and just

like these ghosts you keep helping. You want to get answers about Scott's death and help his ghost, and the harder you try, the more… stubborn you get. It's like you're fixated on accomplishing things, whether it's hauling antiques up your stairs or finding a killer, because you haven't been able to accomplish helping Scott."

Emily slowly put the car in drive and kept her eyes fixed on the street ahead. Was Trevor right? She thought about her sudden independent spirit, and how she had felt when Trevor had offered to help her get the antique mirror up the stairs of Eternal Rest. Her reaction had been almost angry, and she had thought at the time that she didn't need a man to swoop in and save the day for her. But, putting her attitude in the context of her desperation to help Scott, and her frustration at failing to do so, she could understand Trevor's point. Emily felt helpless when it came to Scott, so she was doing her best to fix anything else in her life that she could.

Emily had turned onto the road back to Oak Hill and driven a couple of miles before she finally answered Trevor. "I think you might be right. You might be missing your true calling as a psychologist."

"I'd rather help you solve murder cases than analyze people's brains," Trevor said with conviction.

"You really do enjoy helping bring killers to justice, don't you?"

"I don't know if 'enjoy' is the right word. But, yes, there's a certain satisfaction in—do you hear that?"

Emily did hear it. She felt it, too. The steering wheel pulled under her hands with every *thump-thump*. "Are you kidding me? Do I have a flat tire?" Emily turned on her four-way flashers as she eased her car onto the shoulder of the road. The subdivision the Greenes lived in was far behind them. A few yards away on their side of the road, pine trees loomed menacingly in the growing darkness. On the other side of the road, a field rolled over the hills, and beyond it, Emily could just make out a farmhouse.

Trevor was out of the car and inspecting the tires before Emily had even turned off the ignition. His face was grim as she climbed out and came around to the passenger side.

"Look," he said, crouching down and pointing at a small dark line on the front tire. "You didn't run over a nail or any other sharp object. Someone punctured the wall of the tire."

Emily squatted down and put her fingers against the small cut. "You think someone did this on purpose?"

Trevor stood, glancing uncomfortably at the road behind them as he did so. "Yeah. I think someone followed us to Stella's house and slit your tire while we were talking to her. They made it small, so the tire wouldn't go flat right away. I think they wanted us to get stuck on the side of the road in the middle of nowhere."

Even as Trevor spoke, headlights appeared over the crest of the hill behind them. Emily stood to get a better look at the oncoming vehicle, then instinctively bent her knees so her head was barely peeking over the roof of her car. She could sense Trevor stiffening beside her as the lights came closer.

And then, just as quickly, the lights reached them, and a blue pick-up truck whooshed past.

"Let's get the spare put on as quickly as possible," Emily said. "It's nearly dark."

"That won't help," Trevor said, pointing at the rear tire. "This one is almost flat, too."

Emily swore under her breath. "They cut the tires on this side because the car would have blocked them from being seen by anyone in the house. This is another warning."

"Could Beau have done it? Maybe he's not the sweet

boy Stella thinks he is," Trevor suggested. "He could have easily snuck out to your car while we were talking to her out back."

"It seems risky," Emily said. "How would he explain it to a neighbor who happened to see? My guess is that someone followed us there, slashed my tires, and drove off before anyone could stop them."

"This is a crime. I'm sure your detective friend could send someone out to ask Beau's neighbors if they saw any suspicious activity."

"I need to call Danny, anyway, and fill him in on everything. First, though, I'm calling a tow truck." Emily pulled out her phone, looked at it, then held it high above her head. "Oh, come on! Don't tell me I can't get a signal out here!"

Headlights appeared over the crest of the hill again, but the vehicle was moving much more slowly than the truck had been. It slowed even more as it approached Emily's car, finally pulling off the road and coming to a stop. Nervously, Emily held a hand up to shield her eyes from the glare of the headlights. She squinted, but the lights made it impossible to see what kind of car it was or who was now slamming the driver's side door.

Emily felt a wave of relief flood through her when she heard a man's voice say, "Miss Emily, do you need help?"

"Officer Newton!" As he kept walking toward them, Roger Newton's stocky frame came into view. "We are so glad to see you! Someone slashed two of my tires!"

"Sage called and told me you were breaking the rules. I only wish I had gotten to Beau Greene's house in time to catch whoever did this." Roger was leaning down to examine the rear tire. "You're lucky one of these tires didn't blow completely and send you veering off the road."

Emily shuddered. Scott had died when his car had careened off the road. He had been driving down a straight stretch of a two-lane road at the time, much like the one Emily was on.

"I need a tow truck," Emily said, not wanting to dwell on what could have happened, "but I don't have a signal out here."

"I'll call one for you, but on one condition," Roger said. "No, make that two conditions."

"I'm guessing one of them is that when I get home, I have to stay home," Emily speculated, not able to hide the note of disappointment in her voice.

"Obviously. The second is that you and Trevor ride with me to the station. You can get your car at the garage later."

"What do you need us there for?" Trevor asked warily.

Roger looked at Trevor with disapproval. "I need both of you to tell Detective Hernandez everything you've learned and experienced today. Sage hinted that a lot has been happening. By the way, Trevor, you need to help keep Emily safe, instead of putting her in danger."

Trevor ran his fingers through his hair, and his eyes turned down to the grass. "Sorry. I think Emily and I both underestimated the danger. I never thought someone would sabotage her like this."

"We were about to call Danny to tell him everything," Emily added lamely.

Roger harrumphed grumpily. "Let's go."

Emily and Trevor were ushered into the back seat of Roger's police car. Roger was silent on the drive into Oak Hill, and his passengers followed his example. Emily didn't mind the quiet: she took the time to close her eyes and think. Someone had sabotaged her car. She had been upset about potentially putting Trevor in danger by sending him to track down Wes Gibson, but she now realized that simply asking him to accompany her to Stella's house had been a bad idea. Her need to track down the truth about

Judy and Jerry Bowers had already put a target on Sage's and Reed's backs, and now Emily had drawn Trevor into the fray, as well.

When they reached the police station, Emily and Trevor followed Roger into Danny's office, both of their heads drooping like children who knew they were in trouble. Danny was sitting behind his desk, leaning back in his leather chair with his arms crossed over his chest. "I was supposed to have the day off, you know," he said in greeting.

"Sorry," Emily said quietly.

Danny sat up and folded his hands on the desk. "It's not really your fault," he said thoughtfully. "I mean, it is, because you seem to have stirred up something that otherwise wouldn't be giving us any trouble, but clearly, this is more serious than we realized. I came in this morning because of the library break-in, and then Sage got that note at her shop, and now you're here. Roger told me you decided to play amateur detective, despite my warning. So, tell me what happened."

Emily filled Danny in on every detail, from Trevor's discovery about Beau Greene being Jerry's son to her tires getting slashed. Danny's expression changed from disapproval to worry as Emily reached that part of her story.

"You're lucky it wasn't worse," he said when she finished.

"I know, believe me." Emily was staring down at her hands, which were clamped together tightly in her lap.

"Emily," Danny said gently, "look at me."

Emily complied, looking right into Danny's dark-brown eyes. "I'm not mad," Danny said. "I'm just worried that you're going to get into a bad situation that you can't get yourself out of."

"But it's not just me," she said, feeling tears welling up in her eyes. She silently yelled at herself not to start crying in front of everyone. "I put Sage, Reed, Trevor, and even my guests in danger, too. Just sending Annie and Andy to the library could have had consequences."

"You couldn't have known that," Roger said, unexpectedly coming to Emily's defense. "You thought you were looking into an old murder case that had been solved the very day it happened. You thought your guests were going to learn some Oak Hill history, that's all."

"You're right," Emily agreed.

"And Sage simply wanted to help you communicate with a ghost," Danny added, giving Roger an appreciative nod. "Don't beat yourself up over making the same assumptions the rest of us would have."

"Come on," Roger said. "I'll give you two a ride back to Eternal Rest. Trevor, I don't want you going anywhere other than straight home once we get there. Understand?"

"Yes, sir," Trevor said evenly.

Roger not only drove them back to the house, but he went inside, too. Sage and Emily's guests were in the dining room again, and Sage gave Roger an exaggerated smile when he walked in. "I'm so glad you're here, Officer Newton," she said with a false cheeriness. "I've just received a very threatening phone call."

21

"No, I didn't recognize the voice. It sounded like they were trying to disguise it or maybe even using some sort of voice changer," Sage was saying. Roger was sitting across from her at the dining room table, writing furiously in his small notebook. Sage had already explained she didn't recognize the phone number the caller had used, and she had no idea who it could have been, other than the person who didn't want them delving too deeply into the Bowers twins' murders.

"Did you get a sense of whether the speaker was young or old?" Roger asked, trying a different angle.

"No. Like I said, the voice was too distorted. Besides, the call was so short that I didn't have a lot of time to think about how they sounded. They just said, 'I know you're still looking for answers. Stop it, or you'll be the next target.' They hung up before I even realized what was happening."

Emily was hovering in the doorway, her eyes darting between Sage and the front door. *Who's out there? Are you watching us right now?* She hated feeling so unnerved in her own home.

When Roger was satisfied Sage had told him everything she possibly could, he called Danny. The conversation was brief, and when Roger hung up, he gave Emily a look that was half stern, half teasing. "Detective Hernandez agrees with me that you need adult supervision. I hope you're ready for another guest tonight. He'll be here within an hour."

Emily laughed incredulously. "What, is he going to stay all night?"

"Yes," Roger said without a trace of humor.

"Oh. Okay, well, he can sleep in the empty guest room. I'll change the sheets real quick since Reed slept there last night."

"Nope, I call dibs on that room," Sage said. "Jen and I are going to stay here tonight, too. If I'm getting threats, that means she's also in danger. It's better if we're all together under one roof, especially if there's a detective in our midst."

Instead of responding to Sage, Emily turned to Trevor and said, "Are you staying, too?"

"No, I'm heading home. I promise to call if anything odd happens."

"And I promise to add your house to my patrol route tonight," Roger said, standing. "I'll walk out with you. I want to go home and take a quick nap since it looks like I'll be driving around most of the night."

Emily stepped aside to let Roger pass, then spontaneously reached out and put a hand on his arm to stop him. "Thank you for all you're doing to keep us safe," she said earnestly.

"I just hope we find out who's doing this, Miss Emily."

"Me, too."

Trevor leaned in and gave Emily a quick hug before following Roger. "Call me if you need anything. I mean it," he said.

"I think I'll be safe with my house full of guests. I'm more worried about you. Stay alert, and make sure all your doors are locked."

Trevor gave Emily a little salute. As soon as he and Roger had walked out the door, Emily heard Catherine calling her name from the parlor. The ghost hunters had moved there to let Roger interview Sage without all of them watching, but Emily suspected they had heard every word, anyway.

"So, what now?" Catherine asked. She was nervously winding and unwinding the cord for a pair of headphones.

"Now, I suggest you decide where you want to order dinner from, since we're all staying in tonight. Otherwise" —Emily shrugged—"try to have a nice evening. I think we're perfectly safe here, especially once Detective Hernandez arrives."

The doorbell rang a few minutes later as Emily was giving her guests suggestions for dinner. "There's our knight in shining armor right now!" Emily said as she moved toward the front door.

Danny was standing there on the threshold, but Emily noticed Reed was walking up the steps just behind him. She was so surprised to see him that her greeting to Danny died on her lips. Instead, she looked over his shoulder and said, "Reed, what happened?"

"I can't just stop by for a friendly visit?" Reed's tone was light, but Emily could see the tightness in his face.

Emily waved both men into the parlor, which was so crowded there weren't enough places for everyone to sit. Danny put down the backpack he was carrying and introduced himself to Emily's guests.

"We're ordering pizza again, if you want in," Catherine said. Emily noticed she looked less anxious now that someone from the Oak Hill Police Department was there.

"I want in, too," said Reed. He looked at Emily. "I hope you don't mind if I stay here again tonight."

"Sage and Jen have claimed the available guest room,

I'm afraid. I didn't think you'd be back. You're welcome to stay here, of course, but why do you feel it's necessary?"

"I'm being threatened." Reed nodded toward Danny. "I was going to call the police as soon as I got here. I didn't want to stay at my house a minute longer than I needed to, so I left."

Emily frowned. "Sage got a threatening phone call, too."

"Oh, this wasn't a phone call," Reed said. "I opened my mailbox and found a note that said, *I can see you reading this right now. Stop looking into things that aren't your business.*"

"But, you haven't been looking into the Bowers murders. You were here for that one communication session with Judy's ghost, and that was it." Emily was confused but also angry. It was bad enough someone was threatening the people who were actually trying to find the truth, but Reed simply had the bad luck of being Emily's friend.

"Actually, I have been looking into them," Reed admitted. "I pulled the death certificates for both of them this afternoon. I had hoped for autopsy reports, too, but since everyone assumed they had killed each other, neither twin got one. I'm guessing our mystery stalker was watching me again, and they saw me going into the county office."

"Did you learn anything interesting from the death certificates?" Emily asked.

"Not really," Reed said. "The estimated time of death was four o'clock in the afternoon. Otherwise, the report just confirmed the things we already knew."

"Thanks for checking into it, Reed. I'm sorry it's causing you so much trouble." Emily gestured toward the sofa. "I'll let you and Danny fight it out for who gets the sofa, and who gets the floor."

Danny smiled good-naturedly. "I came prepared! I've

got a sleeping bag in my backpack. You can take the sofa, Reed."

"Great," Emily said, rolling her eyes but failing to look as exasperated as she wanted to. "Once the pizza gets here, it will be a proper sleepover! I'm going up to get the guest room ready for Sage and Jen. Catherine, I'll eat anything that doesn't have mushrooms on it."

Emily actually smiled to herself as she put fresh sheets on the bed in the empty guest room. She didn't like the fact that her friends felt the need to stay under her roof for their own safety, but there was something almost funny about the situation. She had been best friends with Sage for years, but this would be the first time she had stayed at Eternal Rest. If only Emily could forget about the reason her friends were staying with her, she could have enjoyed the full house.

Jen arrived right on the heels of the pizza, armed with a shopping bag and a suitcase. "I brought Sage's stuff, plus I stopped and bought a few bottles of wine," she said, giving Emily a sympathetic smile. "We might as well make the best of it, right? You hanging in there?"

"I'm better now that you've brought us wine!" Emily said, taking the bag from Jen. "Sage is already up there, trying to rest up for whatever tonight brings. When you drop your bag off, can you please let her know dinner is here?"

Jen brought Sage downstairs with her just a few minutes later, and soon the group was spread between the dining room and the parlor. Emily was seated at the dining room table, where Danny was gladly listening to stories about the First Coast Ghost Hunters. Blake and Hal were taking turns enthusiastically describing a paranormal investigation at a haunted beach house.

Emily had just taken a bite of her second slice of pizza when Catherine spoke up. "I think we should head up to our room after we eat. I want to try talking to the Bowers twins again. We can tell them everything that's been going on, and maybe one of them will help us figure out who's running around making threats and slashing tires."

Emily started to laugh, but she nearly choked on her bite of pizza. Danny reached over and gave her a thump on the back. She swallowed and said, "I'm fine. I'm just laughing because we're eating pizza and drinking wine, and now we're going to have a séance. This really *is* a slumber party!"

In addition to the five ghost hunters, Emily now had Sage, Jen, Reed, and Danny at her house. Ten of them would have been a crowd in Jaxon's room, so she suggested to Catherine that they split up. Catherine immediately agreed, but before she could start doling out assignments, Reed volunteered to stay downstairs. "I'm happy to keep an eye on things down here," he assured Catherine.

Andy and Annie offered to keep Reed company, and Emily wondered if Annie's ghost hunting days were numbered. After her strange experiences at Eternal Rest, Annie looked like she might be considering an early retirement.

That left seven of them to squeeze into the bedroom where the mirrors were. It wasn't until they were all there, seated on the floor and the bed, that Emily realized it would have been smarter to simply bring both mirrors downstairs, where there would have been more space for everyone to spread out. She was currently squeezed between Danny and Hal, her shoulders pressed awkwardly against theirs.

Danny leaned his head toward Emily's. "I'm excited about this. I finally get to see Sage in action!"

"I assume I'm not allowed to tell Roger about you participating in this with us?" Emily remembered Danny was very firm about keeping his belief in the supernatural out of his police work. He always said that as a detective, he had to be a skeptic.

"Oh, I'm just guarding all of you," Danny said, giving Emily a lazy smile. "It's not my fault you all trooped up here to look for ghosts."

Sage called for quiet, and the room fell silent. Hal raised one glass to the full-length mirror and placed his tape recorder on the ground just in front of it. Catherine was holding the other glass as well as the handheld mirror. "We're ready," she told Sage confidently.

"Judy and Jerry Bowers, we've come to share everything we have learned today," Sage began, her voice dropping into a lower register. Her eyelids fluttered, and her eyes fixed on a spot somewhere above Emily's head. "We have also come to ask for your help. We believe the man who killed you is now threatening us. We need your help to find him."

The silence continued, Sage's voice the only sound in the room. She talked about the note under her shop door, the phone call she had received, Emily's slashed tires, and the note in Reed's mailbox. Neither one of the ghosts made a sound. "And now," Sage said, "we're worried we are being watched. We may not be safe here in Emily's own home."

Emily almost protested because she felt like Sage was being overly dramatic, but it finally yielded results. A voice spoke a word, and just after, a second, higher voice followed. It said the same word. Sage tried to ask some more questions, but that one-word statement from each ghost was all they got.

Hal quickly downloaded the recording to his laptop so he could flip the audio. "I'll review all of the recording later to see if we got any EVPs. But first..." He hit a button, and a deep voice, followed immediately by a higher voice, said, "Watched." The second voice sounded breathy, almost nervous.

Sage's eyes lit up. "I think we're on to something! Hal, start your tape recorder again!" As soon as he had complied, Sage asked, "Jerry and Judy, that was loud and clear. Thank you! Was somebody watching you before you were killed?"

This time, it was the lower voice that answered, shouting something. Again, Hal immediately reversed the recording. The voice, which Emily assumed was Jerry's, sounded scared and angry. "No peace!"

Sage asked more questions for a solid twenty minutes. There were no more answering voices, and finally, she had to concede that Judy and Jerry might be too worn out to talk any more that night. Hal shuffled to his room, his shoulders drooped, promising to review the recordings for anything the ghosts might have said that was only caught on tape, but he didn't sound optimistic.

Yawning, Sage turned to Emily. "The ghosts aren't the only ones who are tired. I'm worn out, too. Between the threats I've gotten today, seeing my regular clients at the shop, and trying to communicate with these two, I'm out of energy. I'm heading to bed to recharge."

As Sage and Jen headed toward their room, Emily overheard Jen say eagerly, "That was so much fun! I should do more of this stuff with you!"

Emily and Danny returned downstairs to let Andy, Annie, and Reed know what they had experienced. They seemed to feel the same mix of excitement and frustration that Emily was feeling. It was great to get some responses from the ghosts, but their answers only seemed to raise more questions. Who had been watching the twins and why? Had someone been spying on them before murdering them? Had they been watched for a long time, or only on the night of their deaths? Sage had asked all of those questions and more, but unless Hal found some EVPs, they still didn't have the answers.

After Andy and Annie wished the others a good night and went upstairs, Emily retrieved a sheet, a blanket, and a pillow out of the hall closet. She started apologizing as soon as she walked back into the parlor. "It's a good napping sofa, Reed, but it probably won't be comfortable for a full night. It's been reupholstered, of course, but these Victorian sofas were not made for sleeping."

"I'll be fine. Better a stiff neck than whatever the watcher might have in store for me."

Emily shivered. "Oh, don't say that. The watcher. It sounds creepy, like something out of a horror movie." For the first time all day, her mind once again returned to the memory of the entity at the lake.

By the time Emily was done setting up Reed's makeshift bed, Danny had spread his sleeping bag and a small inflatable pillow against the wall beside Emily's desk. "At least let me get you a real pillow!" Emily chided.

"I'm going camping for a week this fall with my nephews. I need the practice," Danny assured her good-naturedly.

"All right. You two sleep well. No staying up late braiding each other's hair!" Emily joked.

"Actually, we were hoping to play light as a feather, stiff as a board," Reed said, deadpan.

Emily groaned in an exaggerated way. "No levitating in my house!" She gave them a wave, then shut the parlor door and headed for her bedroom.

Eternal Rest had never had so many guests at one time. Even though three of those people were friends and one was with the police department, Emily was still thinking of them all as guests. She was eager to make everyone feel at home, and she drifted off to sleep while mentally rationing breakfast items to make sure everyone got at least a little something to eat.

After such a long, strange day, Emily fell quickly into a deep sleep. At four o'clock in the morning, she woke up, not suddenly but slowly, as if someone had been softly calling her name. She listened hard, but there were no sounds in the house. Everyone, she assumed, was fast asleep. Emily thought about turning on the nightstand lamp, then decided not to bother with it. She was convinced something had woken her up, but she didn't feel like she was in any kind of danger. That watchful feeling wasn't there, either. Instead, Emily felt a sense of calm that had been missing all week. It was almost a warm and cozy feeling, and her mind was flooded with memories of being at Eternal Rest as a child, sipping hot cocoa while wrapped up in one of her grandma's knitted afghans on a chilly winter evening. What Emily was feeling at the moment was almost exactly the way she had felt then.

Emily didn't question the feeling. She rolled over, sighed contentedly, and fell back to sleep.

After staying up late in the hopes of talking to Judy and Jerry, Emily had set Sunday morning's breakfast time at nine o'clock. By eight thirty, she had already showered and dressed, and she was ready to prepare breakfast. When she walked into the kitchen, she was startled to see Sage, who had dark circles under her eyes and a half-empty cup of coffee cradled in her hands, seated at the table.

Sage looked up at Emily. "They're back, Em."

Emily poured her own cup of coffee as she let the words sink in. She sat down across from Sage before she finally said, "I know. The ghosts came home around four this morning, didn't they?"

Sage looked surprised, her tired face perking up a little bit. "That's right. How did you know?"

"I woke up then, and I just felt good. Comfortable, content. I almost want to say enveloped."

Sage smiled. "Your skills really are improving if you're able to feel your ghosts like that. I'm proud of you."

Instead of feeling proud herself, Emily was simply curious. "What did they tell you?"

"They found him, Em. Out there, beyond the psychic barrier that surrounds Oak Hill. They found Scott."

"And?" Emily was leaning so far over the table her ponytail slipped over her shoulder, the end nearly dipping into her coffee.

"He's weak. They channeled what they saw to me, and instead of being a solid ghost, he's sort of shimmery. It made me think of a TV channel that's coming through on a bad antenna. He clearly lacks the necessary energy to completely materialize."

"Did the ghosts find out why?"

Sage's face fell, and she reached out to put a hand over one of Emily's. "They saw another entity near him. A dark entity. They think… I think… it's draining his energy and trapping his spirit on this plane for some reason. Scott hasn't crossed over not because he doesn't want to, but because he lacks the energy to do so."

Emily used her free hand to wipe at the tears sliding down her cheeks. She had known Scott needed help—he had channeled that message through Reed's cousin—but hearing more details made her heart ache. "What kind of an entity?" Emily asked.

Sage looked at her sadly. "I think it was the one from the boathouse."

"Okay, but that doesn't answer my question. What is it?"

"I don't know, Em. I got the impression the ghosts were terrified when they saw it, but I'm not even sure they know what it is." Sage squeezed Emily's hand. "I'm sorry. I know this is all hard for you to hear, but it's important. The ghosts got invaluable information. We know now that Scott is weak because something is preying on him. That gives us something to research, at least."

Emily rested an elbow on the table and put her chin in her hand. "Did the ghosts talk to Scott?"

This time, Sage actually looked pleased. "Yes. They told him we're all trying to help, and he told them to keep trying. After that, he disappeared, either because the contact completely drained his energy or because the entity whisked him away. Still, the fact they were able to actually talk to him is huge, Em. Now, Scott knows he's not alone. That's wonderful."

"It is," Emily said. "I'm so worried about him, but I'm also glad that after two years, he can have some hope that we're trying to help him."

Emily looked up at the sound of footsteps overhead. "I need to get breakfast out," she said, rising. "Thanks for telling me all this, Sage. Are you okay?"

"I'm tired. I've been awake since they came home, pondering everything they showed me. I'm actually going back to bed, now that I've had a chance to relay everything to you."

Emily came around the table so she could bend down and hug Sage. As she turned to get breakfast ready, she reminded herself to focus on the positives and not on the horror that Scott was being terrorized by the boathouse entity.

Just as she was putting a carafe of fresh coffee on the sideboard, Emily heard a clatter on the stairs. A moment later, Catherine burst into the dining room, followed by Blake, who was self-consciously looking over his shoulder toward the still-closed parlor door. He was moving much more slowly and quietly than his girlfriend, but they both shared an agitated expression.

"Something is happening! In the big mirror!" Catherine said, so wound up she was out of breath. "Come up right now!" With that, Catherine spun on her heel and proceeded to the stairs. Blake actually had to move out of her way as she strode past.

"I'll wake these two," Blake said reluctantly. "I hate to make them get up, but I think everyone will want to see this."

Emily gave Blake a nod and followed Catherine. As she got to the top of the stairs, she saw a sullen-looking Sage emerging from her bedroom, clearly not happy about having her attempt to go back to sleep foiled. Jen followed, looking like she was up for an adventure. Emily remembered Jen was a morning person, so unlike herself, Jen didn't need a few cups of coffee to get going.

Hal, Andy, and Annie were already in Jaxon's room. Emily sat on the floor near the foot of the bed and stared hard at the full-length mirror. Catherine had been right: something was happening. There were shimmers of light and movement in the glass. Andy had brought a video camera into the room, and he was sitting directly in front of the mirror, filming the whole thing.

Danny and Reed shuffled into the room behind Blake, yawning and looking rumpled. "Morning," Reed mumbled in Emily's direction.

Catherine was seated next to Hal, and she kept her eyes on the mirror as she addressed the group. "Blake and I woke up when we heard that scratching noise again. It was so loud I'm surprised you didn't all come running. We think Judy's ghost was actually trying to get our attention. When we came and stood in front of the mirror, we were seeing what you're seeing now, but there wasn't quite as much going on. It's like Judy is trying to show us something, but it's taking a while for the scene to form."

"That's," Sage began before stopping to yawn widely,

"not unusual, especially if she was really tired after exerting her energy last night. She's probably warming herself up this morning."

"Maybe she needs a cup of coffee," Emily quipped.

"I need one!" Sage responded.

"Catherine, have you been able to make out what these shapes are supposed to be?" Emily asked.

"We think it's people, but it's hard to tell."

The shapes were slowly shifting, moving around in the reflected room, and Emily could see why Catherine assumed the shimmering forms were supposed to be humans. It was almost like the shapes were walking.

Emily waited a few minutes, and when it didn't appear anything was really changing in the mirror, she dashed downstairs to the dining room. She piled coffee cups, spoons, sugar, and milk onto a spare serving tray and grabbed the carafe of coffee, then went upstairs again and began pouring cups for everyone. Hands groped toward the proffered cups while eyes remained riveted to the mirror.

Once everyone had coffee, Emily sat down again. This time, she could see a slight change in the mirror. The shapes had gotten brighter, and they seemed to be contracting, taking on a more defined shape. Over the course of the next five minutes, the shimmery forms continued to evolve until there was no doubt they were human. There were two of them, their legs appearing to be right in the middle of Catherine and Andy's reflections.

One of the forms abruptly fell to the ground and stopped moving. The second form bent at the waist, standing over the first, then straightened as a third shadow-human strode into view. This figure moved oddly, with an exaggerated stride and arms that swung wildly. When it reached the center of the mirror, the form that had still been standing fell backward.

"'He killed me.' I think the first one that fell is Judy. Jerry shot her!" Emily hadn't even realized she was speaking. The thoughts were running through her mind so swiftly they just bubbled right out of her mouth.

"And someone else just came and killed Jerry. That's the 'he' Jerry told us about," Sage added. She tore her eyes away from the mirror long enough to throw Emily an appreciative glance. "Look at you, rolling with your intuition! Well done, Em!"

The mysterious "he" continued walking around the room, the big strides becoming even more exaggerated. "What are you trying to show us, Judy?" Sage asked, exasperated. "Why can't you just tell us who killed Jerry?"

In answer, the figure turned so it looked like it was walking straight at everyone in the room. Its form grew larger, until it became clear it was wearing a wide-brimmed hat. It stomped forward until the entire surface of the mirror was one mass of a bright, shimmering form, and then, suddenly, only the room and ten very startled-looking faces were reflected in it.

23

Catherine and Blake enthusiastically volunteered to stay and keep an eye on the mirror, just in case any odd activity started up again. Their one condition was that someone had to bring their breakfast up to them, and Emily was happy to comply. She still had no idea who could have killed Jerry, but they were, at least, making progress. If nothing else, they had learned that one of the twins had, indeed, killed the other.

The other eight people in the house settled in at the breakfast table, all excitedly discussing what they had just seen. When Reed abruptly stood and walked out of the room, Emily elbowed Sage, who was sitting on her right. "What's with Reed? He just left," she said.

"He's going to answer the front door. Didn't you hear the knock?"

Emily laughed. "No, I didn't! It's so loud in here I never heard it! Who would be coming here in the middle of a Sunday morning?"

Emily was only halfway to the dining room door when Reed came back in, his mouth turned down and his brow furrowed. He gestured to Emily to follow him, then turned and walked to the parlor. Emily was surprised to see Trevor there, standing just to one side of a front window as he peered at the world outside.

"Uh-oh," Emily said. She knew by Trevor's stiff stance that he wasn't there simply to check in on his friends.

Trevor looked quickly at Emily, then shut the curtains. He did the same for the other windows in the room, and the parlor felt eerily gloomy in the sudden dimness. As Emily turned on the lamps, Reed left and returned a moment later with a steaming cup of coffee. Wordlessly, he handed it to Trevor, who accepted it gratefully.

Trevor began to lift the cup to his lips, but his arm was only halfway there when he suddenly stopped. His face took on a pinched expression just before he sneezed. With a frustrated, congested huff, Trevor set his coffee cup down and headed straight for a box of tissues on a side table.

Emily impatiently said, "What's going on, Trevor?"

Trevor finally sat down, and Emily noticed how red and irritated his nose looked. Clearly, this wasn't the first time he had used a tissue that morning. "Oh, are you sick?" she added, pausing halfway to sitting down next to him on the sofa.

"It's my allergies," Trevor said in a nasal tone. "I took an allergy pill, so hopefully I'll feel better soon."

Emily went ahead and sat, relieved Trevor wasn't contagious. Rather, she was curious. "What's blooming that has you so congested?"

"I'm not sneezing because of a plant. I'm sneezing because of what I found on my doorstep this morning."

Reed and Emily leaned forward in sync. "Did you get a warning note, too?" Reed asked.

"I wish that was all," Trevor said flatly. "I got a creepy little doll that looks like you, Emily. There was a piece of twine tied tightly around its neck, and there was a piece of paper attached to the twine. It just read, *Emily is next if you keep asking questions.*"

Emily stared at Trevor, too shocked to even say anything. When she finally realized how silent it was in the room, she didn't respond to Trevor. Instead, she got up and walked into the dining room. "Danny, you need to come here, right now." Emily's voice was terse, and she knew it was shaking. She realized her hands were shaking, too, as the shock wore off and the danger of her situation began to really sink in.

Danny stood immediately as the others stopped talking. Every face turned anxiously to Emily.

"Em…" Sage began.

"You, too." Emily looked around at her guests. "I'll fill you all in shortly, okay? I just need a few minutes to sort some things out."

To Emily's surprise, it was Annie who took charge of the ghost hunters. "We all need to get packed up since we're checking out today. We'll be upstairs, so let us know when you want us to come down."

Emily gave Annie the most gracious smile she could muster in the situation. "Thank you."

Danny and Sage followed Emily into the parlor, and as Emily closed the door for privacy, she noticed Jen had also come along. She didn't mind: she just didn't want to throw her guests into a panic with the news that she was now being threatened, too. Somehow, Emily knew her friends would take the news calmly.

As soon as everyone was gathered around the coffee table, Danny looked expectantly at Emily. "What happened?"

Emily waved an arm toward Trevor, who recognized his cue to retell his story. This time, when he finished, he pointed to a backpack sitting at his feet. "It's in there."

Danny stepped forward. "Hand me the whole backpack. I'll just look at the doll so I don't risk contaminating evidence. Hopefully, we'll find a fingerprint or two on the paper."

Trevor complied, and Danny unzipped the backpack

carefully. He stared inside it for a long time before saying simply, "Oh."

"What?" Emily got up and stood next to Danny so she could see, too. Inside the backpack was exactly what Trevor had described, except so much worse. The little doll was only about six inches tall, roughly sewn out of what looked like burlap. Blue felt had been glued onto the body like a shapeless dress. The hair appeared to have been attached with a hot glue gun, and it was a slightly lighter shade than Emily's. However, like her own hair, this had been pulled back into a ponytail.

It was the face that was the worst, though. A red marker mouth was frozen in a scream, and one blue button eye was hanging loose. More red marker had been drawn to resemble a gruesome eye socket.

Trevor sneezed.

"Bless you," Emily said automatically, her eyes still staring at the awful doll of herself. "Why not just send a note? This seems extreme. And creepy."

Danny peered closer at the doll. "The notes haven't been working, have they? You've all continued poking around for information." He looked pointedly at Emily, and she thought he looked uncannily similar to Roger in that moment.

Trevor sneezed again. "Sorry," he said.

"Is it the hair you're allergic to?" Emily asked.

"That's my guess. It probably came from an animal that makes me sneeze."

Sage rose so she could peer inside the backpack, too. "You see how shiny the hair is? It's probably synthetic. That isn't what Trevor is allergic to."

Jen, who was perched on Emily's desk chair some distance away, said sarcastically, "Sage is a wig expert ever since I made her be in a production of *West Side Story* with me during college."

Emily's head popped up. "When we're past all this, you've got to tell me every detail about Sage doing musical theater! Do you want to take a look at this doll?"

"Absolutely not. I have a thing about dolls, and I certainly don't want to see one that looks like you and was probably made by a murderer." Jen actually rolled the chair back a few inches, putting even more distance between herself and the doll.

Reed, unlike Jen, actually did want to get a glimpse of the doll. While the others had been content simply to look at it, Reed put his face close to the opening of the backpack and inhaled deeply. "The hair might be fake, but I definitely get a whiff of an animal smell. My guess is this doll was made in a house with pets. Dogs, maybe?"

"I've never been allergic to dogs," Trevor said. "I think we might be heading in the right direction, though. I'm allergic to goats. Petting zoos were a nightmare as a kid. I wanted to pet everything, and I paid for it, every time."

Emily laughed as she pictured Trevor roaming through a field, sneezing. Her laugh suddenly turned into a gasp as a memory flashed in her mind. "Trevor, are you allergic to pigs?"

"I have no idea."

"The Nelsons have a bunch of pigs. They live right next door to the Bowers mansion!" Emily brought her hands to her head as she fought to remember everything Jim and Sarah Nelson had said to her when she spoke to them. "They hated the twins; they were straightforward about that."

"Emily," Danny warned, "you're making some very big assumptions. We don't even know if Trevor's allergic reaction is because of pigs."

"It makes sense, though," Emily insisted. "It would have been so easy for Jim to slip over there and kill Jerry."

"Okay," Danny said, crossing his arms and looking at

Emily with an expression of indulgence. "Tell me this, then, what motive would Jim Nelson have had for killing Jerry Bowers?"

"Jim really disliked the twins!" Emily paused as the wind was taken out of her sails. Even she could hear how lame of a murder motive that was. When she spoke again, her voice was much softer. "Oh. I guess everyone disliked the twins. I've disliked people before, and I never felt the need to murder them. You're right. It's extremely unlikely that Jim killed Jerry."

"Good work, Detective," Danny said sarcastically, but one side of his mouth curved up in a smile.

"What do we do now?" Sage asked.

"You," Danny said pointedly, "don't do anything. You go about your day like you normally would."

"You don't want us to try to talk to the ghosts again? Maybe, if we ask them point-blank if Jim Nelson killed them, we'll get an answer."

Danny actually brightened up at the suggestion. "It couldn't hurt, actually. Keep the curtains in the room closed. If this house is being watched, which it probably is, then you don't want to give off any hints that you're still trying to get answers. But, Sage, remember—"

"I know, I know," Sage said, waving a hand impatiently. "Talking to ghosts isn't official police business, and anything we learn isn't admissible as evidence."

"This is why you're my favorite psychic medium in Oak Hill," Danny said in his most charming voice.

"I'm the only psychic medium in Oak Hill, but I'll gladly take the compliment. Let's call the ghost hunters in here and catch them up, shall we? They might want to grab their suitcases and hit the road right away, or they might want to stay a while to help out."

"It's safer for them to leave," Emily noted. "Until we

find out who's responsible for this, I think it's safe to say that anyone under my roof can be considered at risk."

"They're adults. They can make their own decisions," Sage countered.

"Sage is right," Reed spoke up. "We're all here because we want to be, Emily. We want to help, and we want to support you. They might be your guests, but after all they've done to help us get answers this past week, they deserve to be given a choice."

Emily unexpectedly felt tears welling up in her eyes. "I just don't want anything bad to happen to them. I would feel like it's my fault. After my tires went flat yesterday, all I could think of was how bad it could have been if a tire had blown out. I might have swerved off the road into the trees, and it would have been just like…" She stopped, knowing if she finished the sentence, she would start crying. Instead, she said, "It wasn't just me who was in danger yesterday, but Trevor, too."

Reed took Emily's hand and looked into her eyes as he said calmly, "What we're dealing with now has nothing to do with Scott's crash. Which, I should point out, wasn't your fault, either."

Emily gave a little sniff and blinked hard. "Once again, you seem to know what I'm thinking."

"Enough with all the guilt and emotion," Sage said loudly. "The sooner we get to work, the sooner we can all get back to normal!" She threw open the parlor door and marched to the foot of the stairs. From there, she shouted, "Hey, ghost hunters! Get down here!"

Immediately, there was a noise of slamming doors and heavy footsteps. Catherine actually ran down the stairs in her eagerness. Only Annie moved slowly, bringing up the rear at a wary pace.

As Emily had expected, the First Coast Ghost Hunters weren't about to give up the search, even after hearing about the newest threat. When Emily gently suggested that the sooner they left, the sooner they wouldn't have to worry about being in harm's way, all of them except Annie vehemently protested, declaring they would even book another night if they had to.

While Sage laid out her plan to try talking to Judy and Jerry again, Emily saw Jen get up from her spot in the corner. She walked over to Annie, said something quietly in her ear, and the two of them disappeared in the direction of the kitchen.

"I understand you wanting to ask the ghosts about this Jim guy, since you think his pigs might be making Trevor sneeze," Catherine said when Sage finished. "However, don't forget that we saw a re-creation of the murder last night. We saw the twins' bodies on the ground, and that guy in the hat walking around the room all strange. Doesn't that seem like a better lead than Trevor's allergies?"

Hal laughed. "What are we supposed to do? Line up everyone in town and make them show us how they walk?" He paced across the floor, taking big strides while swinging his arms wildly. "Look at me!" he said, changing his voice so it was deep and booming. "I'm stomping around in my big boots looking for someone to kill!"

Everyone laughed, seeming to appreciate the humor in the middle of such a stressful situation, but Emily shouted over all the noise. "Big boots! That's it!"

Danny eyed Emily skeptically. "Do you have another hunch?"

"It's not a hunch! When I visited the Nelsons, Jim was wearing these great big rubber boots for working in the field. Not only does he have pigs, which Trevor is probably allergic to, but he has big boots that likely make him look funny when he walks!"

Danny's eyes narrowed. "Do you really think Jim Nelson might have killed Jerry Bowers?"

Emily nodded decisively. "I really do."

"Okay, then." Danny picked up Trevor's backpack and slung it over his shoulder. "Let's go ask him."

24

Emily's leg was bouncing nervously as she sat in the passenger seat of Danny's pick-up truck. Sage, Jen, and Reed had all asked to come along, but Danny had insisted that only Emily could accompany him, as long as she agreed to stay in the truck.

"You'll know your guess is correct if Jim Nelson comes out of the house in handcuffs," Danny had told her.

As the truck got closer to the Nelson home, Emily began to second-guess herself. "What if I'm wrong?" She spoke quietly, more to herself than to Danny.

"If you're wrong, I tell them I'm sorry to have bothered them and wish them a nice Sunday afternoon," Danny said. He didn't sound at all worried, and Emily wondered how he could stay so calm when he was about to confront a murderer.

A possible murderer, Emily corrected herself. There was still no actual proof Jim had killed Jerry. In fact, Danny had said the only reason he was letting Emily go along was because this wasn't a formal visit. As Danny was fond of reminding her and Sage, spirit communication couldn't be used as police evidence. Neither, Danny had added wryly, could someone's allergies.

As they reached downtown Oak Hill, Danny stopped at

the police station to drop off Trevor's backpack. Emily waited impatiently in the truck, and even though Danny was only inside the station for a matter of minutes, it felt like an entire afternoon to Emily. She was anxious to know if she was right. If she was wrong, then whoever was threatening her and her friends might take more drastic measures. It was impossible to hide the fact that Emily was, despite the warnings, still trying to find Jerry's killer.

Emily saw the creepy doll in her mind, and she shut her eyes instinctively. That only served to bring the doll into sharper focus, so she opened her eyes and stared at the front of the police station. She began to count the bricks in the facade, trying to push both the thought and the image of the doll out of her mind.

Soon, Danny came back and began the short, final stretch of the drive to the Nelson home. As they pulled into the driveway, Danny looked over at Emily. "Remember, you stay put. This shouldn't take long."

Danny left the engine running since the day was shaping up to be a hot one, and the air conditioner kept the cab of the truck from being stifling. Emily thought briefly of the lake and how it would again be crowded with people swimming and enjoying the sunshine. *Why can't my life be that simple?*

Emily watched as Danny rang the doorbell and was shortly let into the house. As the minutes passed, she stared at the front door, desperately wanting to know what was transpiring inside. A glance at the clock on the dash showed that only five minutes had passed since Danny had gone into the house.

Five minutes after that, Danny and Jim both walked onto the front porch.

Jim was not in handcuffs. In fact, Emily noticed he seemed to be smiling, and he and Danny were nodding and gesturing to each other as if they were simply having a casual conversation.

Emily felt her stomach tighten. She had been wrong. She had sent Danny into someone's home to accuse them of murder, and she had been absolutely wrong in her assumption. Emily's cheeks burned as a wave of embarrassment and even shame swept over her. What would Danny say? Even worse, how much of this news would become Oak Hill gossip?

Danny and Jim shook hands, and Danny turned to descend the curving staircase. His friendly smile disappeared the second his back was to Jim. When he climbed into the truck, he was quiet.

"I'm so sorry," Emily began. "I really thought—"

"I think so, too," Danny interrupted.

"What? But you two walked out onto the porch like a couple of old friends!"

"Yeah, because Jim didn't say anything to make me think your hunch is correct."

"Didn't you just say you agreed with me?"

Danny turned to Emily. "I did, and I do. Jim seemed genuinely confused when I mentioned threats. Plus, he didn't give me the impression he was trying to hide anything. It was what I saw on his back deck that made me think he's just a very good liar. There were several burlap sacks out there, like the material that doll was made from."

"Let me guess: feed bags for the pigs."

"Probably. But I can't arrest a guy because he has empty bags that may or may not be tied to our case. We'll have to keep digging for evidence. And, of course, when I say 'we,' I mean me and the Oak Hill Police Department. You're not out of danger until we resolve this, so I don't want you so much as going to the grocery store without letting me know about it first."

Emily's embarrassment about being wrong had now shifted to worry about being right. If Jim was guilty, then he would double his efforts to threaten Emily, or worse. As Emily stared at the house, wondering if she was more in need of a bodyguard than an assistant, she watched absently as Jim appeared in the distance, walking from the barn that stood on one side of the backyard toward the house. He had a wide sun hat on and a bucket in one hand.

Jim was taking long strides, and Emily could see big black boots moving up and down, up and down across the tall grass. Even the swinging arms matched the vision from the mirror perfectly.

Emily sat up straighter. *How could Jim be coming from the barn, if he had just been inside the house with Danny?* Slowly, the idea taking shape even as she spoke, Emily said, "Judy and Jerry died in the middle of winter. The killer was probably bundled up. If they were wearing a heavy jacket and the same big boots and hat Jim always wears, it would have been easy for the twins to mistake the person for Jim."

Emily opened the truck door and hopped out. She began walking toward the house as Danny hurried to follow. He put a hand on her arm, gently trying to hold her back. "Emily, what are you doing?"

"You said Jim didn't act like someone with something to hide. Let's see if his wife acts differently."

"Jerry said 'he' when talking about his murder."

"And I just thought that was Jim walking from the barn to the house, but it couldn't be him. Back on the night of the murders, Jerry had just shot his sister. I imagine that in the moment, all Jerry saw was boots, a jacket, and a hat, and he recognized all three as belonging to Jim. He made the same mistake I just made, and he died before he realized who had really stabbed him."

Emily had reached the stairs, and Danny's grip on her

arm tightened. "You know how this works," he said sternly. "I talk. You sit in the car."

"How about I just stand behind you?"

"Fine, but if someone tries to attack you later, I get to say 'I told you so.'"

"Deal." Emily stepped back to let Danny lead the way up the stairs.

Jim seemed surprised when he answered the door to see Danny there again, and he seemed even more surprised when he spotted Emily. "Back for more detective work?" He tried to laugh, but his smile turned into a grimace.

"Actually, I'd like to speak to your wife, please," Danny answered crisply, all trace of his former friendliness to Jim gone.

A muscle twitched in Jim's cheek. "Sure." He waved Danny and Emily inside while calling, "Sarah?"

Sarah was just coming through the sliding glass door that led onto the back deck. Looking past her, Emily couldn't see any sign of the burlap feed bags, and she wondered if Sarah had hidden them away.

Danny didn't go for a polite line of questioning like he said he had used with Jim. He looked at Sarah frankly and asked, "Did you kill Jerry Bowers?"

Sarah set her mouth firmly and crossed her arms over her chest. She had taken off her rubber boots on the deck, and she looked slightly funny as she planted her socked feet in a wide stance.

"I knew it," Jim muttered.

"Knew what?" Danny asked, his eyes flicking to him.

"All these years, I've wondered if it was her. She had been out in the field all afternoon, until the cop cars started showing up next door. When she came inside, she wasn't wearing my jacket anymore. She swore she had never put it on in the first place, and I'd just lost it. But I wondered,

175

even then, if she hadn't buried it somewhere because it had blood on it." Jim had been addressing Danny, but he turned his whole body toward his wife, his face sad. "You were always watching them. So often, I'd come home from work and find you out in the field, hanging over the fence, staring at that house. You couldn't get enough of their drama."

Watched. No peace. Judy and Jerry's words echoed in Emily's mind.

"How did you know?" Sarah's voice was defiant. She wasn't looking at her husband, though. Her eyes were pinned on Emily.

"The ghost of Judy Bowers showed me," Emily said evenly, even though she was fighting the urge to turn and run away from Sarah's glowering stare.

Sarah gave a short laugh. "You think a judge is going to go for that?"

"I think a judge will be interested in comparing the feed bags to the doll you made," Danny said. "I also think an analysis of the doll will show traces of pig dander."

Sarah's face twisted. "I knew you were going to be trouble," she spat at Emily. "For twenty years, this town has been happy to tell the sordid tale of the twins who killed each other. No one ever questioned that. Why did you have to go looking for the truth?"

"Why did you kill him?" Danny pressed.

Sarah's face crumpled. "I didn't mean to. Really. I heard the gunshot, so I went over to investigate. The front door was unlocked, and I found them in the bedroom. Judy was on the floor, bleeding, and Jerry had a gun in his hand. When he heard me come in, he swung the gun toward me. I panicked and grabbed a pair of sewing scissors off the vanity. I stabbed him." Sarah shrugged. "He would have killed me. It was self-defense."

"And what about Judy? She was still alive when you

killed Jerry, wasn't she?" Emily knew it was the only way Judy could have shown the re-creation of Jerry's murder in the mirror: she must have witnessed it before she died.

Anger clouded Sarah's face again. "That awful woman asked me to help her. But, with Jerry dead, that meant she would inherit the house. She'd sell the land and build condos. It would have changed the zoning in this neighborhood, and I would have had to get rid of my pigs. Besides, who wants to live next door to something like that? We didn't buy this house so we could have a hundred neighbors right next door!"

"What did you do to Judy?" Emily asked.

"I didn't do anything." Sarah crossed her arms again.

"You just stood there and let her bleed to death?" Emily's mouth felt dry, and she tried to swallow.

Sarah merely gazed back at Emily, refusing to say more.

Danny pulled a pair of handcuffs from his pocket and took a step toward Sarah.

"It was self-defense!" she cried, stepping back so she was against the sliding glass door. One hand snaked behind her.

"Judy Bowers might have lived if you had helped," Danny said. "The police report also said that when they found the twins, the gun was on the bed, nowhere near where Jerry's body was. He didn't have the gun in his hand when you walked in, did he, Sarah? You didn't kill him in self-defense."

Sarah slid the door open and turned to run. Danny was on her in seconds, tackling her to the floor of the deck. She howled as Danny put her in handcuffs, declaring that their neighborhood was better off for what she'd done. As Danny led her back into the house and sat her down on the couch, he was listing the other charges that would be brought against her. "You threatened people with violence, you slashed a car's tires—"

Sarah gave Emily another venomous look. "I should have run you off the road instead."

Danny called for a squad car to come collect Sarah. While they waited for the officers to arrive, Jim stood awkwardly behind the sofa. "After Emily's visit, and her questions, you were suddenly gone so much," he said, looking at his wife as if she had tried to kill him rather than the next-door neighbors. "I woke up Friday night, and you weren't in bed. You weren't even home! It made me more suspicious than ever, but I never thought you were out trying to hurt other people. Weren't the twins enough?"

Poor guy, Emily thought. *It must be awful to suspect your own wife of murder. It must be even worse to find out you're right.*

Soon, there was a knock on the door, and Danny let in two officers Emily didn't recognize. They hauled Sarah away, then Danny turned apologetically to Jim. "I'll need you to come to the station, too. I know this is a lot to take in."

Jim nodded, looking slightly dazed. He drove himself, following Danny's truck. On the way to the station, Emily suggested she call Sage to come pick her up, but Danny shook his head and sighed impatiently. "You're involved in this case. You're not going anywhere until we've gotten your statement, too."

Emily felt like she was being chastised. "I'm sorry," she said quietly.

Danny seemed to realize his error. He reached over and squeezed Emily's hand. "You did great," he said kindly. "I'm not upset that you helped us solve a murder, especially when we didn't even know there was a murder to be solved! I just don't like the fact that you keep putting yourself in danger. First, that artist tried to poison you, and now this…"

"I'm not a fan of it, either," Emily said. "But I know you understand how important it is to me that I help these ghosts."

"I know. That's why I'm not telling you to stop. I'm only asking you to be careful."

"Thanks for letting me come along today, Danny."

"Thanks for cracking the case."

By the time Emily finally got home on Sunday, the sun was already sliding behind the oak trees in Hilltop Cemetery. After giving her statement, she had called Sage to come pick her up. Sage and Jen had peppered Emily with questions on the entire drive from the police department back to Eternal Rest, but Emily simply kept repeating her promise to tell everyone everything as soon as they arrived.

Emily was actually surprised to see that "everyone" included her guests. She had assumed they would have already started their drive home, but instead, they had opted to wait until they could learn what had happened during the confrontation with Jim Nelson.

Feeling exhausted but satisfied—and finally safe— Emily rallied what energy she had left to tell her entire story in detail. Sage shut her eyes and shook her head in horrified disgust as Emily described Sarah's confession that she had stood there and watched Judy bleed to death.

"Now I know why that room felt so wrong when we used to sneak into the place as teenagers," Reed said. He turned to Sage. "And now you know why your clients who bought the mansion can't sleep in that room."

"Hopefully, now that we know the truth, we can cleanse the room of any negative energy that's left in there," Sage said, nodding. "No wonder that room feels so dark and oppressive! Of course, I've also heard rumors that old Mr. Bowers didn't actually die of natural causes…"

"No!" Emily said, waving her hands to ward off Sage's suggestion. "I am not diving into another possible murder. No, thank you!"

"No, you're not," Sage said firmly. "You've got more important work to do right now. We have to find out who or what is keeping Scott's spirit too weak to cross the barrier."

"Right now, the most important thing we can do is cross over Judy and Jerry Bowers," Emily corrected. "Hal, Trevor, can you two please bring the mirrors downstairs? We'll all meet you in the backyard."

"Why are we going outside?" Catherine asked.

"You'll see," Emily promised.

Emily went to the old barn behind the house and grabbed a dirty tarp that Reed and his team often used when working on plots at Hilltop. She spread it on the grass near the back porch light, then directed Hal and Trevor to put the mirrors on top of it when they came out. Everyone formed a loose circle around the mirrors, but all eyes were on Emily.

"Sage, can you please let Judy and Jerry know that the person responsible for both of their deaths has been arrested?" Emily decided not to pass along Stella's message for Jerry. Instead, she hoped his journey to the next phase of his existence might be a fresh start.

Sage cleared her throat, took in a deep breath, and closed her eyes. "Judy and Jerry Bowers, your spirits have been waiting for so long on this plane. Your patience has paid off. Sarah Nelson has confessed to killing you, Jerry. She also confessed to letting you die, Judy, instead of helping you or calling an ambulance. She has been arrested, and she will go to jail. The truth is known, and justice will be served. You can both cross over now. You should see a light and hear the voices of your loved ones calling to you. Follow that light and be at peace."

When Sage finished speaking, the sound of crickets filled up the long silence. Eventually, Annie squeaked, "Are they gone?"

"I'm not sure, to tell the truth," Sage said, walking up to the full-length mirror and peering into the glass. "You there, Judy?"

"I have a backup plan," Emily said. She reached down and grabbed the hammer that she had also gotten out of the barn. "I know it's seven years of bad luck if you break a mirror, but I don't care. I'd rather risk bad luck than not do everything I can to give the twins peace. They might have been horrible people, but they didn't deserve to die the way they did. They didn't deserve to have their spirits trapped for so long, either."

Sage stepped back, smiling at Emily approvingly. "It's a nonsense superstition, anyway. I don't think you have to worry. Who knows? Maybe it will even bring you some good luck!"

Emily stepped forward and swung the hammer hard against the full-length mirror. The glass turned into a spiderweb of cracks, then shards began to tinkle to the ground. She gave it another solid smack for good measure before turning her attention to the handheld mirror. She winced as the hammer shattered the antique glass. *I'll call Trish later and apologize for destroying this beautiful gift from her aunt.*

"Oh!" Sage said. "Em, you did it! I just sensed their presence, only for a split second before they moved on. I could feel their relief and gratitude."

Emily beamed at Sage.

Catherine sighed heavily. "We'd better hit the road.

We've got a five-hour drive back to Jacksonville, and we all have to get up and go to work tomorrow."

"Thanks for an unforgettable stay, Emily," Hal said. He stepped up to Emily and hugged her tightly.

Once Hal released her, Emily turned to her guests. "And thanks to all of you. We couldn't have helped the twins without your efforts."

Trevor and Reed volunteered to clean up the broken glass, so Emily escorted her guests inside the house. As they walked, she saw Annie approach Jen and overheard her say, "Thanks for the pep talk earlier."

Jen gave Annie an understanding smile. "I know it can get scary sometimes, but you're in safe hands with your friends. Sage taught me that trick when we first started dating, and it really helps."

The First Coast Ghost Hunters had already loaded their two cars, so all that was left was for them to thank Emily again and say good-bye. Every single one of them insisted on giving Emily a hug, even Hal, who said that once wasn't enough. Finally, though, they were in their cars and on their way.

The house felt strangely empty without them, and Emily was grateful she had Sage, Jen, Reed, and Trevor all there with her to keep her from feeling lonely. Often, Emily was happy to be alone once guests checked out. After such an intense few days, though, she welcomed the company of good friends.

Sage told Emily to stay put on the parlor sofa while she got a bottle of wine and glasses, and Emily was happy to comply. She took advantage of Sage's absence to ask Jen, "What were you and Annie talking about? I heard you tell her Sage taught you something."

"When Sage told me she was a psychic medium, I was a little freaked out by the idea. I had these crazy visions of a ghost tagging along on one of our dates and then coming home with me. She taught me a chant—I guess it's almost like a spell or a ritual—for spiritual protection. I repeat it to myself whenever I feel nervous about what might be out there in the unseen world." Jen smiled contentedly. "Of course, I've gotten so used to what Sage does for a living that it hardly ever scares me anymore. I could tell everything was getting to Annie, so I took her aside and taught her the chant."

"She's a sweet girl, but I expect she does the ghost hunting just to keep Andy happy," Emily said.

Jen looked surprised. "Oh, do you not know? Annie actually has some mediumship abilities. She said she fought it for a long time, but she's slowly trying to learn to use her gift. I think that's why she got scared by the twins. She perceived their presence in a way the other ghost hunters couldn't."

Emily's expression matched Jen's. "Wow. I had no idea. But then, I think we've established that I don't always know what secrets my guests are hiding."

Jen laughed. "Well, at least Annie hasn't murdered anyone!"

"That we know of!" Emily pointed out, joining in the laughter.

Emily enjoyed the evening with her friends. She had guests coming on Monday, but she could wait until the morning to clean the guest rooms.

Finally, reluctantly, everyone headed home. Jen, Trevor, and Reed all had to be up early the next morning for work, and Sage admitted she was mentally exhausted after all of her work with ghosts during the previous few days. "Remember, Em," Sage said as she hugged Emily tightly, "I also had that long chat with your resident ghosts when they came home. I need to recharge so I can help my clients at the shop tomorrow."

"I know. Thanks for all your help, with Scott and the twins."

"We'll figure out what that dark entity is, and, more importantly, how to release its hold on Scott."

"We will," Emily said confidently.

Trevor was the last to leave, and Emily walked with him onto the front porch. "The next time you want to buy heavy antiques," he said, "don't call me for help moving them. Instead, just don't buy the stuff at all, okay?" He winked at Emily.

"Thanks a lot!" she called sarcastically as he descended the porch steps. Trevor just gave a wave and kept walking to his car.

Once the taillights of Trevor's car had disappeared around the curve in the road, Emily leaned against a porch column and looked out at the dark sky. A restless breeze stirred the leaves of the dogwood trees planted on either side of the steps, and it smelled faintly like rain was coming.

Emily had been so exhausted earlier, but after Sage's words about her ghosts, she was wide awake, thinking about the things they had relayed to Sage about Scott and the entity that was pursuing him. Knowing that going to bed would be fruitless, Emily went inside and retrieved her flashlight and the key to the cemetery gate.

It was rare for Emily to go to the cemetery alone at night, but it never felt spooky. The place was so familiar to her that it simply felt like taking a walk around her own yard. Emily unlocked the gate and walked up the main path that led to the top of the hill. Once she reached the summit, she sat down on a bench in front of a granite mausoleum. She could see stars peering down between the branches of the oak trees overhead and a dim glow on the Western horizon from the lights of the next town over.

Emily's eyes were directed upward, but a shimmer from

the direction of the lights caught her attention. She peered hard at the tops of the trees below her.

Probably just a firefly.

No, there it was again: a little shimmer of golden light that stretched into a thin vertical line before disappearing. It was no firefly.

At first, Emily thought the light was close, but as it appeared and disappeared a few more times, she realized it was far away, hovering above the trees beyond the stone fence that surrounded the cemetery.

The shimmering light appeared again, stretching even farther in a vertical line before disappearing. As it stretched, it took on a gently curved shape.

Emily kept her eyes fixed on the spot. For a few minutes, everything remained dark. Then, fainter than before, the light appeared again. This time, the point split into lines that reached toward the earth, forming an outline that was definitely human.

It was nearly half an hour before the light appeared again. Emily was just about to give up and go back to the house when she spotted it. The human shape shimmered into existence, and, faintly, Emily could see a face take form. The details were hazy, but even from so far away, one detail stood out in bright clarity: a shining pair of green eyes.

The eyes disappeared so quickly that for a moment, Emily doubted whether she had really seen them. She closed her eyes briefly, thinking of Sage's constant advice to her. "What does my intuition tell me?" Emily whispered.

The answer came to her mind, loud and clear. Those green eyes were Scott's, and she had caught a glimpse of his ghost, materializing beyond the psychic barrier that surrounded Oak Hill.

"I see you, Scott," Emily said, smiling even as tears ran

down her cheeks. "I see you, and we're going to help you. Keep fighting. I love you."

Emily sat on the bench for another two hours, but Scott never appeared again. Maybe his energy was spent, or the entity was preventing him from materializing. Nevertheless, Emily felt happy and hopeful. Scott was getting stronger, and after two years, she had finally seen him.

As she walked back to Eternal Rest, a gentle rain began to fall. The drops against her face felt cleansing, washing away the fear and uncertainty of the past week. Emily sighed. "I guess Sage was right," she told herself. "Breaking those mirrors today really was good luck!"

A NOTE FROM THE AUTHOR

Thank you for reading *Scenic Views!* And, as always, thank you for supporting indie authors like me. Will you please leave a review before you go? It really helps!

Thank you,

Beth

ACKNOWLEDGMENTS

I wouldn't have made it this far in the series without an amazing group of people. Jena at BookMojo brings the design and marketing skills, and Lia and Nicole are my trusted editors. Not only do my test readers catch plot holes and errors, but they also provide unending moral support. Thank you Brenda, David, Kristine, Lisa, Mom, and Sabrina.

NEXT IN THE SERIES

**Find out what's next for
Emily, Sage, and the ghosts of
Eternal Rest Bed and Breakfast!**

Breakfast Included

ETERNAL REST BED AND BREAKFAST BOOK FIVE

PARANORMAL COZY MYSTERIES

Grainy Day Bakery's biscuits are to die for.

Dead bodies are expected in cemeteries, but not simply thrown into an open grave. The newspaper's notorious food reviewer had plenty of enemies in the small town of Oak Hill, Georgia. Unfortunately, it's Emily Buchanan's good friend Trish who is the prime suspect since the biscuits that killed him came from her bakery.

As Emily tries to balance running Eternal Rest Bed and Breakfast and working to bring her late husband's spirit home, she also has to help clear Trish's name. After all, someone Emily knows and trusts could never be a killer... could she?

BOOKS BY BETH DOLGNER

The Eternal Rest Bed and Breakfast Series
Paranormal Cozy Mystery
Sweet Dreams
Late Checkout
Picture Perfect
Scenic Views
Breakfast Included
Groups Welcome
Quiet Nights

The Betty Boo, Ghost Hunter Series
Paranormal Romance
Ghost of a Threat
Ghost of a Whisper
Ghost of a Memory
Ghost of a Hope

The Nightmare, Arizona Series
Paranormal Cozy Mystery
Homicide at the Haunted House
Drowning at the Diner
Slaying at the Saloon
Murder at the Motel
Poisoning at the Party
Clawing at the Corral

Manifest
Young Adult Steampunk
A Talent for Death
Young Adult Urban Fantasy

Non-Fiction
Georgia Spirits and Specters
Everyday Voodoo

ABOUT THE AUTHOR

Beth Dolgner writes paranormal fiction and nonfiction. Her interest in things that go bump in the night really took off on a trip to Savannah, Georgia, so it's fitting that her first series—Betty Boo, Ghost Hunter—takes place in that spooky city. Beth also writes paranormal nonfiction, including her first book, *Georgia Spirits and Specters*, which is a collection of Georgia ghost stories.

Beth and her husband, Ed, live in Tucson, Arizona. Their Victorian bungalow is possibly haunted, but it's not nearly as exciting as the ghostly activity at Eternal Rest Bed and Breakfast.

Beth also enjoys giving presentations on Victorian death and mourning traditions as well as Victorian Spiritualism. She has been a volunteer at an historic cemetery, a ghost tour guide, and a paranormal investigator. Beth likes to think of it all as research for her books.

Keep up with Beth and sign up for her newsletter at
BethDolgner.com